"I won't say any [...] she promised. She turned toward the mirror again. "Do you think there's a chance Jake never loved me?"

Tears flooded her eyes.

"Why would you ask that?" Missy gently gripped her shoulder.

"He was always the romantic one, Missy. The guy who could look out at the vast horizon at the edge of this property and not be frightened by it. Jake used to believe in me, and then he left, and I thought I had worked through that rejection." She shook her head, and teardrops marched down her cheek like sad little soldiers. "Why does this still hurt?"

It was strange the way some wounds only scabbed over in life but never truly healed. They simply mended enough so a person could put one foot in front of the other and call it resilience.

Cassie looked toward the ceiling and mumbled, "He didn't care as much as I did."

"That can't be true," Missy responded. But she didn't say anything else.

Praise for Laura Elizabeth

"*THE RELUCTANT COWBOY* gave me all the feels with sweet romance, drama that made me gasp, and a twist on the classic second chance trope. I loved it!"

~Suzanne Baltsar, Author

~*~

"Spend some time with Jake and fall in love with a reluctant cowboy. With her sensitive and deft writing, Laura transports readers to a land where family triumphs over distance, dreams aren't easily forgotten, and some old secrets can't stay buried. Don't miss a chance to spend time there."

~Elizabeth Newman, Reader

The Reluctant Cowboy

by

Laura Elizabeth

A Second Chance Romance Novel

The Reluctant Cowboy

Cover Art by *Kim Mendoza*

The Wild Rose Press, Inc.
PO Box 708
Adams Basin, NY 14410-0708
Visit us at www.thewildrosepress.com

Publishing History
First Champagne Rose Edition, 2020
Trade Paperback ISBN 978-1-5092-3287-1
Digital ISBN 978-1-5092-3288-8

A Second Chance Romance Novel
Published in the United States of America

Dedication

This book is dedicated to my Mom and Dad,
who never thought being a writer
was a frivolous pursuit,
and to my very own reluctant cowboy, Nicholas,
who inspired me to write a broken man
with a heart of gold.

Chapter One

Jake

Jake Smith left Cherry County for a reason.

Still, his gut hurt over that choice. The ache in his lower belly was warm, nagging—a real pain in the figurative ass. Nothing worked to soothe it.

He pulled off the road to witness the late spring sunset from what had once been his favorite spot near the old Smith Ranch. Other parts of America didn't have the same sky as Lovestruck, Nebraska did. He'd traveled to enough places by now to know for sure. Purple, orange, and pink brushed across the blue of dusk where, in the distance, a small church and cemetery rested on the horizon.

He shuddered at the tainted masterpiece of the hillside as he gulped the last of his diet soda, crunching the can afterward and tossing it onto the passenger seat. A gas station sandwich wrapper and a banana peel already lay discarded. Yesterday, he'd finished his stunt work in an A-list film and had a week to eat whatever he wanted until protein shakes and fish were his constant menu items again. He savored the dark soda aftertaste sticky on his tongue before he started up his steel gray Lexus.

It was reckoning time.

The crunch under his tires was harsh but familiar,

despite his seven years away from his hometown. He slid his hand through his hair—damp from sweat and a very real sensation he was going to be sick.

Sunnybrook Dude Ranch and Inn.

A hokey cowboy boot sign hung at the entrance of the land his family used to own. In big white letters, the sign proclaimed his great granddaddy's place was now an inn with a small dude ranch attached, owned by one Miss Cassie Sullivan. The last part he'd learned from his sister three months ago, when she'd asked him to walk her down the aisle. Jake was a hardened man, but a "pretty please" beg from Missy was one of his Achilles heels. He had a couple more. For instance, Cassie's name, even the thought of it, sent a shiver through him, and names shouldn't do that.

Think of this as another stunt job, he reminded himself. Terrifying. Dangerous. Doable. He'd used the same pep talk for a month straight, and he still couldn't commit to it, except for maybe the "terrifying" and "dangerous" parts. He was on a wild bull, holding on for dear life. Why did he have the feeling he'd end up on his ass?

Water stung his eyes, but he sniffed emotion away. He parked his Lexus next to the inn, kicking at the paved sidewalk that used to be dirt on his pathway to the door. His Sperry shoes scratched against the black tar as if there was a ball-and-chain attached to his ankles.

He gripped the brass knob. Was he supposed to walk inside with his tail between his legs or his head held high? He'd made something of himself abandoning this place. It wasn't like he'd run away to become a nobody. In another part of the country, he was a kind-of celebrity. In Lovestruck, he was infamous.

A small bell jingled as he finally trudged inside the house. He dropped his brown leather bag onto the wooden floor. Daily he'd done the same thing when he'd come home from school. Now, however, the door was brown instead of black. It creaked less than it used to.

Jake glanced around the entryway. Yellow wallpaper with daisies covered the walls, along with family pictures. Each frame had a brass plaque under it naming the various Smith family members like museum artifacts. Maroon and purple flowers wrapped around the banister leading upstairs in honor of Missy's wedding on Saturday. His sister was getting married. Who was the guy good enough for her? No was good enough.

"No one," he muttered.

After years of distancing himself from his family, he hadn't lost his ability to worry about Missy.

The check-in desk was an old, scratched-up wooden table where his brother, Frankie, had studied during their school years. A heart with Cassie's and Jake's initials inside it scarred the wood. He ran his hand over the etching, remembering when he'd carved it. It was like touching the top of a casket, not quite as melodramatic, but not so far off, either.

He clasped the edges of the desk to keep steady, rocking from his heels to his toes. His fingers knocked into a tarnished bell, with the words, *"ring for sex,"* on it. He stared at the stupid little thing as he grunted, "You've got to be shitting me."

"You said a bad word," a school-aged girl coloring

in the corner said. She didn't look at him. He was about to ask her to find someone, but a woman rushed in from the kitchen.

"My apologies. I'm helping bake pies tonight along with managing front desk duties. I must have missed the bell. I told my boss we needed something louder."

"Maybe a rooster would do," he answered.

"That's funny, sir." The young lady had powder on her cheek, even as she tried to wipe it away. She smiled. She was at least a decade younger than him and staring as if she had a chance at his cold heart. Jake never reckoned he understood women's tastes well. Apparently, grumpy, has-been cowboys were her type.

He glanced at the "My name is" sticker on her chest. "*Anna,* I'm here for the Smith/Larkins wedding."

Anna gazed at his jawline for a breath longer before finally looking at the laptop in front of her.

"Last name?" she asked airily.

He rolled his eyes. "Smith. My name is Jake Smith."

She bit her bottom lip, and the little girl in the corner looked up. The kid smiled and capped her marker.

"Smith. Smith. Smith." She giggled. "S-m-i-t-h."

"Jake Smith," Anna said. "Of course. We're used to seeing Frankie around here more often now."

"That can't be right," he said flatly. His older brother rarely visited Lovestruck. He'd left to be the big shot, city-slicker type he'd idolized in the business magazines. Did Frankie suddenly appreciate the beauty of his hometown or was his financial career in the shitter?

He would never admit out loud he hoped for the

latter. All those dreams Frankie chased had left little time to appreciate the work Jake and his dad put into ranching. Like he wasn't proud of what his family had built from the ground up. Frankie had once told him that shoveling cow manure was not the way he was fixing to make a living. It wasn't long afterward when Frankie's dialect changed and "fixing" was no longer part of his vocabulary.

Was their mom's health declining? Was that why his brother returned more often to a town he'd skedaddled from as soon as he could?

Jake's chest tightened, and he rubbed his covered pecs. Maybe after their dad's passing, Frankie had a change of heart about his loyalties. He was the oldest Smith son, after all.

Anna scrambled through a stack of files, handing him a baby blue packet when she'd found it. "Here's your information about the next couple of days."

The papers were bulky enough to be a damn screenplay. However, Missy was the only girl in the Smith family, so his mother and Cassie had likely gone through every detail meticulously. Missy deserved every second of it. Their family had been through a lot.

Nostalgia tore through him just as grief did, only his form of nostalgia was more like remembering what could have been. Sometimes in the middle of the night at home in Los Angeles, his dreams lingered on Cassie and this place. More than once, he'd jolted awake with tears in his eyes and a hard-on ready to pound the memories where they belonged.

"You'll be staying in one of the tents behind the house." Anna's words knocked him back to reality.

"What?" He'd barely noticed the tents when he

walked in minutes ago. They were blackened peaks which could've been mistaken for small pine trees. Not a place to plop his ass this weekend.

"Most of the guests are staying in them," Anna explained.

That part made sense. The only decent hotel he remembered was twenty miles from Lovestruck. Missy would want her family closer, especially with the packet she'd prepared.

"But I'm the brother of the bride." He ran his hand through his hair. He'd forgotten to get it cut. Maybe the barbershop on Main Street still existed. He'd check it out in the morning before he was scheduled to pick up his suit, as his packet indicated in big, bold letters.

"Yes, sir. That doesn't change what my boss has arranged." Anna tried to further sell him with, "Cassie paid out of her rear to get the finest vendor to install the tents. You'll love it."

He was stuck on the *Cassie's rear* part of Anna's sentence because—what a thought. Her ass was once curved in a way that constantly made him want to grab her if only to produce the sweet, flirty yelp and kiss she'd gifted him with in return. Her kisses were sweet with the promise of naughty. There wasn't one kiss he'd forgotten.

He tightened his fists.

Anna gazed at his body as her hands braced the desk. Her tongue darted between her lips like she was attempting to catch a frog.

Ribbit.

Poor girl. All the lust in her eyes, and he wasn't the one to tame it. That didn't mean he wouldn't use it to his advantage.

He leaned forward and rung the "ring for sex" bell again as he winked. His shirt sleeves were buttoned at his elbows, showing off his forearms—one of his stronger physical attributes.

He had other accomplishments, too. After years of doing hard stunt work, he was a man who'd dated the "it" producer of the day's niece; a bloke who people paid big bucks to so that A-list stars looked like they were jumping off buildings.

"Help me out here. There must be something you can do," Jake said.

She tucked a strand of brown hair behind her ear and glanced away. His hope deflated. It was no more of her decision to send him outside than his.

"Look, Miss—"

"Just Anna."

Jake nodded. "Look, Anna, I'm a thirty-one-year-old man who prefers to sleep in a house. *My* house."

"It's not your house anymore, Jake."

A quiet, but firm voice behind him sent a wave of heat from his forehead to the bottom of his feet. He jumped, not because he hadn't sensed in his gut that Cassie was approaching moments before she spoke, but because her energy scared the shit out of him. She had a way of walking—a light, dominant energy that he recognized. Even now. His skin filled with goosebumps, and his heart beats sped at least five seconds ago. Sweat formed along his forehead.

God, make her look awful.

He turned around.

No prayer was answered that Cassie had become a hag. If anything, she'd managed the impossible by becoming even more beautiful. Jake stared at her after years of not allowing himself to even imagine her for too long. Her cleavage played peek-a-boo in a red strappy dress with daisies on it. A teal horseshoe necklace, probably one she'd made herself along with the dress, rested on her clavicle. The memories he hadn't wanted to surface—this time of a younger Cassie at the kitchen table crafting her jewelry and clothing, pretending to be at home in Nebraska—came back to him anyway.

Why had she stayed?

"Ahem," Cassie said, but he wasn't done taking her in. Sweet mercy. His gaze roamed downward to the place where her dress stopped at her knees. Her legs were tan and still had the muscle tone of a woman who loved exploring Lovestruck's landscape. When he'd first met her, she'd been Cassandra from Connecticut. A politician's daughter who was supposed to go back to where she came from after the summer was over. Apparently, she never did.

"Is there a problem?"

She even had a little accent now. It was the cutest, most repulsive thing.

His fists clenched at his sides again. "Cassandra."

"It's still Cassie."

"Cassie" had been the nickname he'd given to her. Not entirely original, but she'd loved the shortened moniker and had held onto it, apparently.

She smirked, and he was about to smile—thinking they were having a moment—when she added, "And the tent is still where you're staying."

Cassie bit her bottom lip.

He blinked.

They were suddenly younger people again, Cassie

in his arms, doing her lip biting thing to convince him that her way was best. Was she doing the same thing now? He swore away more images about who they once were to each other, and how much he'd once believed she was magic incarnate.

"You sure do have a mighty big stick up you're a"— He glanced at the little girl still in the corner— "behind."

"Aren't you charming," Cassie answered, clearly ignoring the fact he was being a gentleman and not cussing in front of the child.

He clenched his jaw.

"And just as hardheaded as ever seeing you didn't call to rent a room. You're lucky you're even getting a tent."

She straightened the name badge she wore, proclaiming her title. It may as well have said "Boss Lady" instead of "Manager." Her vibe would've been sexy if it hadn't ruined his argument. Jake never could win an argument with her.

"Politician's daughter." He coughed under his breath.

"What did you say?" She crossed her arms.

He ignored her rhetorical question. "I take it those tents are where you're staying, too?"

Cassie clicked her tongue, as if calculating her words—it never boded well for men when women did that. He straightened as if he'd been asked to do so.

"I'm staying at the old ranch hand's house, which is my house now. I run this place, Jake. Everything." The words sounded sadder than a woman on a successful career high. Still, she looked too beautiful to warrant sympathy. Her rich mother was probably funneling her cash to keep the ranch afloat, although the place appeared to need several updates. Much of it was the same homey space it had always been.

"I'm sorry you don't prefer your accommodations, but perhaps next time you could at least call to make a reservation. I had to guess you were coming, despite the busy Hollywood man you are nowadays." Cassie looked him up and down, and not in the way he wished she would—with regret that, as MC Hammer put it, she couldn't touch this. "You're mighty successful, but you should've had your assistant at least contact us."

"I don't have a—" Jake stopped. He did have an assistant. No use in lying about how different his life was now.

Cassie leaned over the counter. "I like the Sperry's."

"They're comfortable."

"They're not you, Jake."

"To hell with your judgment, Cassie. You don't know me anymore." He didn't mean to cuss. He'd been successful until his slipup.

He distracted himself from her glare by looking anywhere but her face. When he returned his gaze, Cassie's shoulders had softened.

"You're right. I don't know you."

The truth of her confirmation hit him like a bull's eye.

"But that's not my fault, Jake. You left all by yourself."

That wasn't exactly what happened. It wasn't even *how* it happened.

"Those are rough pastures you're going down," Jake warned.

She shook her head. "Sunny, can you come help me?"

The timidity in Cassie's voice didn't match the woman he once knew, and he scowled—sadly and despite himself—wondering what other ways she'd changed.

A cell phone rang an old Elvis song, and Cassie reached into her front dress pocket, snapping her fingers gently at the little girl still at the table. This time, the little girl followed Cassie, whispering that Jake had cursed in front of her.

Cassie turned toward him and looked back at the girl. Sunny. "I'll make him put a dollar in the jar tomorrow."

Like hell she would.

"Anna, my decision stands about the tent," Cassie said to her desk lady. Her attention turned to her call. She rested her hand on her forehead, as if rubbing out a headache, and with her phone propped between her shoulder and ear, she glanced at him once more before nearly stomping toward the room that used to be his dad's den. Now, it had a sign on the door that read Inn Management. The lobby chilled when she left.

Despite his awakened frustration with Cassie, his body reacted with a different frustration altogether. He was half-hard and covered in goosebumps. His gut ache turned into a yearning, which was worse than a gut ache, if you were keeping record.

Anna stood behind the desk, mouth agape at the heated exchange between exes, though she likely understood little about their intimate history. He wanted to knock on the closed door and force Cassie to converse with him. That would mean he'd have to talk, too, which sounded like climbing a damn mountain at this point.

"What tent am I in?"

"Twelve," she answered, almost mechanically. "We have numbered posts outside each."

He was already halfway out the door when she continued. "It's next to the big one. Your brother rented it and gave his room to Mr. Fisher, who just had hip surgery." There was girly wonder in her voice as she added, "Frankie's such a great guy."

Anna's words hit him in the ass, along with the door, on his way outside.

Frankie had become the town's hero?

What damn movie set had he traipsed onto this weekend? And Christ almighty, how was he going to get through the next forty-eight hours?

Chapter Two

Jake

For the nth time in three hours, Jake growled against his pillow, throwing his fist into it. The sound was like a baseball entering a mitt square on.

He'd already thrown his second pillow across the tent because the extra plush reminded him he was in his thirties and had no one—not even the prospect of a woman—to share his tent with for the weekend. Pun intended. The actual tent wasn't bad as far as outdoor living spaces went. There was a pop-up bed and two battery-operated lanterns on makeshift nightstands, aka fancy milk crates; complimentary water and snacks in a wicker basket in the corner; and, potpourri. They'd even set up fancy port-o-johns outside the tents, which were nicer than some of the bathrooms in the houses around Lovestruck.

Was he glamping?

If anyone saw this sorry display of outdoorsmanship—him snuggled in a full-ass bed in a tent—he'd have to fight rattlesnakes for the next year to earn back cred. He made his living by being the guy who understood ruggedness. He despised himself for succumbing to glamping.

And for letting his anger overwhelm him.

He'd learned in therapy to return to the present

when any emotion got the best of him and allow the emotion to pass. He breathed in and out deeply, fisting his pillow again. At *present*, his knee, still hurt from his last stuntman-related injury. His nerves pricked his skin like a bee sting. Jumping from buildings was getting harder. He attempted to believe his bodily pain had nothing to do with being in Lovestruck. Still, the throbbing in his head from replaying his exchange with Cassie made sleep as rough as lassoing the moon. Speaking of the moon, he'd forgotten how bright it shown over the ranch. The light bled through the thin fabric of his humble abode. Tonight, it wasn't keeping him company; tonight, it was highlighting every ache.

He got up and put on his jeans. No use ruminating for another four hours when he could wander around *his* childhood home without interruption. Outside his tent, he stared at the sky, which was as clear as Cassie's eyes had been dark earlier in the evening. He may've been angry, but there were details a man could still appreciate.

How had he ever forgotten how pretty her brown eyes were—the color of his once favorite thing—the ground. Earth. Land. In truth, he hadn't forgotten. He'd suppressed any and every detail he could about the life he'd left. A man couldn't restart his damn path by remembering the reasons he should've stayed on a different one.

Insects chirped and a light breeze made the grasses beyond the camping area sound like something lurked in the shadows. Whispered voices inside Frankie's tent turned into muffled laughs, then smacking lips, and finally heady, desperate sighs.

Jake had enough of the outdoors.

The light in the ranch house's kitchen was dim. He trudged across the mowed yard, accidentally tromping on budding spiderwort. The pinkish color of the three-petal flower was purple in the night.

He remembered his mom had once scolded him for traipsing on her garden.

She'd cried over her ruined shrubs.

Jake rubbed his chest. He'd been such a shit.

He opened the back door, groaning at the smell of some sort of egg bake. Bacon sizzled. The white wallpaper with bundles of cherries still hung from when he'd lived on the property. The kitchen was like walking into a bakery. The space was small but as warm and welcoming as always.

Especially with *her* sitting in front of him.

"Hi, Mom," he rasped, his limbs getting heavier with the gravity of seeing her.

"If it isn't my boy."

Her voice tugged at his heart. Although he'd been more of his father's son, he couldn't deny the soft spot he had toward his mother, too—likely because she was the first person who knew he existed. If he ever became a dad, he yearned to hold his child first and often thereafter. Fatherhood and ranching. Those had been his aspirations.

"Jake," his mom urged. She sat at a rectangular kitchen table, braiding brown twine around small bouquets of sunflowers. She didn't stand, but she eyed the matching wooden bench across from her. "Sit so I can get a better look at you. I see you've grown out your hair to look like a caveman's."

He cleared his throat like he was in trouble.

She spared him, glancing at the knot she was

making. "Sunny said you were here in the flesh."

"The kid said I was here?" He narrowed his eyes, ignoring her comment about his hair. He'd remembered Cassie calling the little girl Sunny. He'd also noticed she resembled Cassie, but he blissfully ignored the fact until now. He'd never explored what his ex had done in the intimacy department after he'd left. At the most, he'd pretended that she'd joined a monastery or sworn herself to celibacy. She could've at least hightailed it out of his childhood town to start a different life. He could deal with her ghost in Lovestruck. He wasn't sure about seeing her again. It was all sorts of wrong.

"Her exact words were '*The* Jake Smith' is here," his mom said.

Jake chuckled. "You say it like I'm an urban legend."

"Aren't you?" She raised an eyebrow and smirked. "A legend, that is. Jumping off trains and buildings."

He sat and stared at her. She didn't appear ill, so there was no reason for Frankie to visit Lovestruck more often in her regard. Something in his chest loosened. His mom existed. She was talking and breathing in the same room as him. And she was still radiant with shoulder-length hair that was now silvery blonde. Her glasses held her bangs back, and her cheekbones were more defined than seven years ago. As he examined her, taking in how the years showed in the small creases near her eyes, he shook his head, almost muttering his guilt out loud. Years he couldn't get back; years he could've spent with one parent, even though he'd lost the other one too soon. His leg twitched as if he needed to move—to run. He kept his ass planted instead. He still had a weekend to survive.

"It's not glamorous," he said.

"Your last film did well. How'd you jump from the hotel?"

He adjusted his seat on the bench. "You watched my movie?"

The nearest theater was an hour away and unless she'd slowed down, the travel time would cut into her active life of volunteering and mothering everyone in Lovestruck. Then again, she'd do anything for her kids, even let them run away and abandon every promise they'd made to take over the family ranch. To do movies, no less.

Apparently, Cassie had stepped in to save the day.

His nostrils flared, but he didn't say anything.

"We've seen all your movies, Jake."

He figured the "we" was his mother and Sophie Cristian, her best friend and owner of I Do Boutique on Main Street. His mom and Sophie had done everything together just like Missy and Cassie when she'd visited Lovestruck the late spring and summer months after their third year of college. Missy always brought friends home with her during the summers; she was bored on the ranch otherwise. After her first year, she'd brought home Amanda from Texas. After her sophomore year, she'd brought home Sahara from San Diego. After her junior year, Cassandra Sullivan had arrived. Jake had assumed she would take on the role of an additional little sister like the others. *W-r-o-n-g-o.*

"It's a dangerous business you're in." His mom interrupted his thoughts.

"It hasn't killed me yet."

She flinched.

He shook his head. "Sorry, Mom."

Death wasn't something to joke about to anyone around here. Still, he was possessive of how brutal it was. Even the town's heroine, Bridget Smith, wrapped up in being everything to everyone in Lovestruck, had a life outside of Matthew Smith. That wasn't true for Jake. Not back when he'd needed direction.

"I promise I'm careful." He absentmindedly picked up some of the twine and braided it. He'd lost track of how many days he'd braided his sister's hair when they were younger. Frankie had teased him about it, but Jake enjoyed time with his sister—telling her what to look for in a man as she got older; telling her he'd kick anyone's ass who tried to hurt her. Trot forward…he hadn't met Missy's fiancé yet. How had their relationship ended up like it had, with her having to track him down through his agent?

Things didn't feel as screwed up in Los Angeles, so naturally he preferred to ride on back there as soon as possible. The boulder on his chest was too heavy tonight. He'd take the smog of the city over this shit any day.

"Cat got your tongue?"

"Just thinking."

His mom pursed her lips. "I understand better than you do why you left."

How could she possibly know the identity crisis he'd faced when his dad died?

"Mom, I—" He stopped. The years between then and now didn't matter anymore. He would be back in California in a couple days. This was already a more cordial meeting with her than he expected. Why ruin the peace with the truth?

"Never mind." He helped his mom complete the

centerpieces until exhaustion finally tugged at him like a nagging dog.

"Have you seen Cassie yet?" his mom asked as his ass left the bench.

He fumbled down again. Court was not adjourned, apparently.

"Briefly," he answered. "Long enough to confirm what Missy told me when she'd invited me to the wedding. Cassie runs this place now. She must've taken after her mother—politicking her way into the town's heart; taking over Dad's land; becoming little miss authority."

His mom reached across the table and patted his hand. "I didn't raise you to be mean. You of all people know how hard Cassie's family situation hurt her."

He remembered. When Cassie's mother's affair had come out nationally the winter prior to Cassie's visit, the scandal had ruined her family. From what she'd ever told him, she'd had a complicated relationship with her mother even prior to the public fallout. Jake hadn't been able to imagine the Sullivan family's dysfunction.

Life had a way of humbling a person.

"I'm just being a dick, Mom."

His mom muttered something about his language. She added, "No. You're being a man who still has feelings for his ex."

"Cassie?" He scoffed. His feelings for her included attraction because she was tragically beautiful, but real I-need-this-woman feelings? How could he have those when he didn't know her anymore? He'd lived without her for seven years.

"Are you kidding me? Cassandra Sullivan?"

"No, Norma Therese. She has a picture of you over her television set." His mother rolled her eyes playfully.

Jake knocked his knuckles against the table. Norma was an elderly lady who had helped his mom garden back in the day. She'd also taken to pinching his ass every time she saw him. If not his ass, then his face. The woman had a serious thing for pinching.

"She's still around?" he asked.

"Yes, and she's coming to the wedding, so consider yourself warned."

He cleared his throat. "I'm sorry things happened the way they did."

His mom stood. "We still have the dude ranch. Bless Cassie for doing it all on her own."

"She learned from the best." Jake nodded toward his mom, who'd likely helped Cassie as she built the dude ranch out of the family's property.

She put a tea kettle on the stove and muttered over her shoulder. "No, son, I think she takes after you."

That felt like a compliment he didn't deserve.

Chapter Three

Cassie

"Dammit." Cassie winced, setting the needle into the pincushion on her wrist. I Do Boutique was lit with antique lamps, which gave the space a pinkish, feminine glow. Gray and purple area carpets covered the wooden floors. A gold bird cage housing a real finch kept her company.

Cassie checked her poked finger for injury.

"Dammit," she repeated.

Luckily, there was no blood and no Sunny around to tell mommy to put a dollar into the curse jar. Her almost seven-year-old daughter was gleefully helping Bridget tie ribbons around the napkin sets for Missy and Parker's reception.

Cassie needed a break from wedding setup. Today, she'd awoken before the horses to put finishing touches on the wooden tables Matthew Smith had built the same summer Cassie fell in love with his middle son. She'd also milked the few cows still on the ranch, checked the chickens, and plucked the weeds near the inn's back door. She'd cursed at whomever trampled over her spiderwort.

This routine in Lovestruck—her routine—was what she'd loved most when she first arrived at twenty-one-years-old. The other major perk had been spending extra moments with Missy's brother, Jake.

Jacob Hunter Smith.

That summer, he'd been a guilty pleasure fantasy to a city girl like her. He still was, even if last night's exchange with him hadn't gone as smooth as buttercream.

She'd replayed the scene over after Sunny went to bed. Jake was stubborn as ever—arguing with her about a tent.

She smiled.

Jake's tent.

The playful innuendo turned sour as her thoughts moved to his current attitude toward her. They'd camped together twice. He liked camping. She hadn't forgotten how cherished Jake had made her feel under the stars. No man since him had made her feel that way.

Now, he had a lot of other feelings toward her and none of them were particularly conducive to playing nice for the weekend. Which really sucked because there were things—important things—she needed to tell him. To be fair, it wasn't only *his* attitude disrupting civility. She'd also picked a fight about his Sperry's, and she'd savored the fire in his eyes afterward. He wasn't indifferent after seven years.

Since Jake's RSVP card had arrived with "yes" to Missy's wedding—a yes Missy probably begged him for—Cassie had lived in denial he'd show up, especially when he never made a reservation for the inn. When Bridget had asked her how she felt about his pending homecoming, she'd shrugged any emotion away. It had been seven years, for heaven's sake. Love didn't linger around for seven years. She was fine. She was an adult woman who had bigger things to worry about than her first heartbreak. She'd listened to all the sad songs long ago.

"*Fair point*," she said, fist pumping the air.

Now, however, she'd actually seen Jake, and her observations were messing with her.

Her fist retreated. Victory lost.

First off, he was more attractive than ever, transforming from boy-next-door-adorable to rugged-and-Herculean. He was beautiful in all ways—fantasy-worthy, unfortunately.

Too bad she also hated him. A pure, deep-in-her-core hate borne out of her deepest fear realized—abandonment.

"I really do hate him," she said to the finch.

He fluttered his wings. Obviously, the bird was on her side.

She finished stitching Missy's hanky, biting her lip as distraction. She had to pee. Her lower belly ached from bladder pressure, It was one of the changes her post-partum body never recovered from wholly. She couldn't hold anything anymore. A good joke; a sappy commercial. They were instigators to many a pee-in-her-panties moments.

She glanced at the wooden clock on the wall. Six minutes until Jake was scheduled to pick up his suit. Way too long to live in misery. She set her work down and scurried to the bathroom.

Mid-stream, the bells jingled over the storefront door.

"Be right there," Cassie shouted as she rolled her eyes. In true Jake fashion, he'd arrived at eight fifty-five. She'd hoped his promptness had changed, given how late he'd shown up in Lovestruck. He'd missed a whole day of games and merriment—three pages of Missy's Packet of Fun. But the dude couldn't give a woman time to relieve herself.

"Were there always so many bells in this town?" Jake asked as Cassie came out of the restroom near the back of the store.

"You're early." She crossed her arms.

He ran his hand through his enviable locks. "I tried to get into the barbershop before I came here."

"He's closed on Friday's."

Jake dropped his hand. "I know."

She hoped the barber was too busy to cut his hair tomorrow. Jake's tresses were golden and untamed. Her throat filled with saliva she had to swallow, along with her pride. She still enjoyed the physical ambience of Jacob Smith.

To be fair, no woman in her right mind would disagree that he was gorgeous. This had nothing to do with anything dormant inside her.

Absolutely nothing.

The sun cast shadows across his figure, making him look bigger than last night. Cassie drank him in, and most of her anger diminished—an unfair power he had over her. He'd probably already run or done whatever he did to achieve his threaded arms, currently on display in a blue button-up shirt. He also wore dark jeans and those Sperry's—Sperry's—that sounded like heavy thunder as he walked further into the boutique. His face had lost the innocent baby fat he'd once had. In its place was a chiseled jaw unshaven from last night. His aviator sunglasses held back his unruly hair.

He was a large presence. Too large.

His suit wasn't going to fit.

She dusted the glass countertop in the center of the room as he approached it. "I'm glad you're in a tolerable mood this morning. Maybe sleeping in a tent agrees with you, after all?"

Jake seemed to ignore the question, asking, "Why are you here?"

"I work here."

He rubbed his forehead as if she'd given him mind-blowing information. "So you run a dude ranch, you're basically planning my sister's wedding, and you work at a bridal boutique. Are you also the mayor or does that job still belong to Mrs. Parks?"

Cassie reluctantly relished his husky voice. He sounded the same as he used to, like an old folk singer with crackly, low pipes.

"There aren't enough hours in the day for town domination on top of everything else I have to do. I'm exhausted."

Exhausted was an understatement.

She stopped dusting and fiddled with a stack of receipts. "Ms. Cristian wanted extra time with her granddaughter this morning, so she asked me to fill in."

"Dana had a kid?" Jake referred to Sophie Cristian's only child.

Cassie leaned in. "She sure did. The daddy is Mark Banks from Kensington Park."

"Ah, she betrayed Lovestruck and went to the dark side." He mocked the longstanding rivalry between the two towns, mostly because of how good both high school football teams were each fall season.

"We're still forgiving her." She winked.

He chuckled, glancing around the space and resting his gaze on the finch. "I guess it's nice of you to help out."

"I am nice." She tossed a dust rag at him. It hit his chest and fell to the floor. "I'm a lot of good things, Jake."

The truth was she also needed any extra money to pay down the debt from running a failing dude ranch she hadn't brought herself to sell. This was the life she fought for, despite the email she'd received a couple weeks ago from Missy's friend, Heidi, who was looking for a brand developer for her new bridal line. The opportunity was in New York. Cassie hadn't considered the job seriously at first. Still, the idea of it lingered strongly in her thoughts, popping up daily like a comic strip dialogue bubble.

"You always were a harder worker than you had to be," Jake said.

She blew hair off her face. "What's that supposed to mean?"

He leaned his toned forearm onto the counter. "With your mom being the political queen she was and you going to all those fancy, private schools—"

"I met your sister at college, Jake."

"Yeah, well, Missy went to a fancy college," he said. "She worked her ass off to get there."

Cassie crossed her arms. "And I didn't?"

He put up his hands. "I'm not fixing to offend you."

He sounded like he actually meant his sorry excuse.

"You're never trying to do anything, are you, Jake?"

"I just meant you never *needed* to work all that hard." He shook his head at her now gaping mouth.

"But you always were a hard worker. It's one of the things I admired most—I'm screwing this all up."

He stopped. Smart man.

His damn dimple on his left cheek was as maddening as ever. She wanted to say so much to him. He'd hurt her. Abandoned her. She'd hurt him, too, but with how unaffected he was in seeing her again, she suddenly doubted her news would be all that devastating anymore.

"Surely you're not here to go over my résumé." She changed the subject. "I'm assuming you're looking for your suit."

He knocked on the counter. "Yes, ma'am."

"Did you seriously just 'ma'am' me?"

His eyebrows pulled together.

Confused was not a cute expression on any man, especially one who had the newfound ability to irritate her every two seconds.

"Fine, *Mr.* Smith, I'll go get your suit."

His eyes widened, and he turned ghostly white.

"Cassie." His voice was a warning.

She endured the same gut-punch. Jake's dad was Mr. Smith. The only Mr. Smith. Not even Frankie could go by it without a certain silence filling the room. Cassie had trodden on a subject that still affected them. Her mouth fell open as she diverted her eyes. She cleared her throat to apologize but retrieved his suit instead, dropping the conversation as a small olive branch to him. When she returned, his color was back.

"That jacket—" His forehead tightened as he took the clothing, his fingers brushing hers.

She ignored the spreading shiver his touch created over her arm and across her chest.

"It's going to be a little snug," she finished for him. *In the width of his back, near his shoulders. In the ass area. Along his waistband and groin.* Okay, the suit was not going to fit him anywhere.

"You've become a man, cowboy. Your mother sorely misjudged that when she gave me your measurements."

Cassie had dreamed about those measurements since she'd received them. How would Jake look bigger and broader in the flesh? Devastatingly handsome was the answer. He stood before her, and he was so attractive.

And mad.

Jake huffed. "Mom could've called me."

She dropped her arms. "She did. *Several* times. You didn't call her back since it wasn't her birthday or a holiday."

"I've called her more than that."

"Oh, one other time a year?" Cassie held up a finger to accentuate just how little once a year more was. "What is the matter with you?"

Something flashed across Jake's eyes. Regret? Bitterness? More anger? Humor that she'd scolded him? She smirked at her last thought. Jake could still boil her blood.

"The suit will work. Great talking to you, sassy Cassie." He attempted to b-line it toward the storefront's door, using his nickname for her when they'd fight as younger adults. He likely hadn't realized he'd said it.

"Oh, no, you don't." Cassie caught up to him and spread her arms across the doorway, blocking him with her body. He scanned her face, staring as if he was about to say something. He stopped himself like a horse on a cliff. Good. Cassie didn't prefer to remind Jake that he had already disappointed his family enough over the past seven years. He was going to behave this weekend. She would do her part to ensure it. Missy deserved her family together.

"Jake." She annunciated her next words slowly. "Try it on. Now."

The stand-off that came afterward was one for the movies. She refused to budge. Her hands dropped to her hips, and she glared at him. Her eyes watered, desperate to blink, but she would win this battle, so help her by-golly.

"You're a damn pain, Sullivan." He stomped determinedly into one of the three dressing rooms and yanked the white sheet across its track for privacy. The harsh noise was like a whistle being blown at the end of a football game.

Victory.

She held up her arms like goalposts and blinked a dozen times to get her eyes working properly again. She imagined him undressing ten feet away, and her breaths shortened. This moment was as close to being with Jake naked as she would ever get again. He hadn't come home in seven years. His absence proved where she ranked on his list of important memories.

She stood behind the counter with her co-worker, Lauren, who'd come into the store during Jake's second grunting meltdown.

"You okay in there?"

"Just dandy." Jake sounded winded.

"How long does it take a stuntman to put on a suit?" she joked to Lauren.

The sheet slid across its track again, and Jake emerged.

Cassie and Lauren snort-laughed at the spectacle.

Jake's arms were stuck in an almost scarecrow position as the suit's fabric strained to cover the man underneath it. Only one button was done on his ivory shirt. The clasp of his waistband hung undone, revealing navy boxer-briefs. His taste for underwear hadn't changed. Nor had Cassie's taste of underwear on him, given the way her legs brushed together when she scanned every part of his physique.

She gulped at the barely contained outline of his groin, and Lauren, clearly ogling at the same area, dropped her spoon into her yogurt container. A speck of food hit Cassie's lip, and she licked it away.

"Is there anything we can do? Sew extra fabric into it or something?" Jake asked.

"We're not magicians." Cassie stepped closer to Jake, taking his arm and guiding him to the small, circular platform surrounded by mirrors on three sides. Her voice caught as she stared at their reflections together. Jake's Adam's apple bobbed. Her hand on him dropped to her side, making them look like the famous Grant Wood painting, *American Gothic*, where the farmer couple appeared downright depressed.

What could have been.

Lauren brought up a similarly gray suit from a wedding that had never happened. Cassie recognized it immediately.

"Could Jake use Fran—"

"Yes," Cassie answered, grabbing the suit and waving off Lauren's confused look. This wasn't the time to walk down that road. Not when she nor Jake had spoken kindly to each other for more than ten minutes since he arrived last night. She couldn't casually explain to him how she'd ended up staying in Lovestruck.

"Try this on." She kept her voice steady and eyed Lauren again. Her co-worker clearly got the bite-your-tongue memo and went back to eating her breakfast at the counter.

Cassie rubbed her forehead. Things had been so complicated at one point in her life. At least she'd done something right and rooted herself in Lovestruck instead of where Sunny's dad had wanted her to be.

"Cassie."

She snapped back to reality. "Yeah?"

Jake held out his hand. "I need the suit."

Cassie still clutched it tightly. She handed it to him and turned toward the breakroom, needing a minute— or an hour—to collect herself.

She'd tried visiting Jake in California once. She'd taken the flight; she'd written one hundred different versions of the truth on airplane napkins. But she never left her hotel room once she'd arrived. When she had gotten the courage to phone him instead, his agent answered. Jake was at a premiere with "a very pretty woman." The call had ended abruptly.

She'd rather have Jake angry with her for making the ranch into a dude ranch than for breaking his heart in another way altogether.

****

Ten minutes later, she was on her knees with pins in her mouth as she marked where Jake's pants needed to be taken out. More than once, he moved his weight from one foot to the other.

31

"Sh-top doin' 'hat," Cassie said when one particular weight shift moved his groin too close to her mouth. His waistband needed an alteration. It wasn't like she was trying to torture them both with her proximity to his manhood.

He exhaled. When she glanced up, he was staring intensely into the mirror.

"What?" He flicked his gaze down.

"Nice view o' yoursh-elf in the mirror?" A pin dropped from her gritted teeth. "You're handsome. Get over yourself."

He dropped his arms. "Sorry if I don't know where to look, given where your head is."

She didn't need to be reminded. Cassie was an adult, and yet she reacted to him as if she had never experienced a hardcore crush, which was not true. She had plenty of boy band posters on her wall until she got to Lovestruck. One poster, in particular, had inspired her first good vibration.

"You're such a guy," she retorted.

"And you're such a—ah—Christ Almighty."

She'd stuck him on his upper thigh. Nothing to draw blood—just to get him to shut up. She stopped. Two new customers—a bride-to-be and her mother— were looking at dresses. She couldn't cause a scene in front of them.

Cassie stood too quickly and nearly toppled onto the floor. Jake caught her with one arm, but she pulled away to circle his backside, which did nothing for her dry throat or dizziness. His shoulders were broad; his waist small; his legs long, lean, and muscled. What a torturous view.

She picked lint from his covered shoulder to slow

her rapid heartbeats. Still, even though it was the simplest, most platonic of touches, her breaths quickened.

They made eye contact in the mirror again. This time, he smiled—almost shyly. His gaze fell to her lips.

She gripped his shoulders, wishing their history was different so this moment could feel like a second chance. Like a small step toward forgiveness. She glanced at his chest, rising and falling dramatically.

Her anger had turned to hurt somewhere in the past seven years. Time was a powerful thing. She longed to smack Jake upside the head for severing their relationship. But she still ached to kiss him.

Jake turned toward her.

Her hand dropped as his fingers held her arm. He stepped down from the platform, bumping against her chest. She didn't step away. He licked his bottom lip and stared at her.

"What are you doing?"

"I'm trying to get through this just like you are," he answered.

"That's not—"

"Cass." Lauren rushed to the dressing room from the supply room, phone in hand.

Cassie jumped. She hadn't heard the phone ring. "What?"

She tucked wisps of hair behind her ears and straightened her outfit, wiping any Jake-ness off with her palms. No harm, no foul. Her fellow employee didn't seem to notice her off-behavior. In fact, the concern in Lauren's eyes made her stomach drop.

She broke into an instant sweat.

"What is it?" Jake asked, simultaneous to Cassie's,

"Is Sunny okay?"

She nearly shook Lauren for not responding fast enough. If her daughter was hurt—

"A cow." Lauren's voice was an octave higher than normal.

Cassie went over every scenario involving Sunny and a cow. None of them were good.

"Lauren."

"Mr. Karl's cow got out, and the barn was open and…" She gulped. "It's in the barn."

"My barn?" The same barn that Missy's guests would be snacking in this afternoon and having dinner in later? The same barn she'd spent a week re-arranging from its usual education center?

"Well, did you leave the barn doors open, Cassie?"

She backhanded Jake on the chest. It was almost easy to ignore how tight and perfect his pecs were when he was annoying.

"The groom's dinner is set up in there for tonight, Jake."

His eyes widened. "Shit."

"Yeah."

Maybe like a stuntman or maybe like a cowboy, Jake grabbed her hand as they sprang into action and dashed outside.

Chapter Four

Jake

"I walked to work this morning," Cassie explained, emotion clear in her voice as she shouted that they'd have to take his car.

He pointed to his Lexus, and they hopped inside.

Cassie glanced at the shiny gadgets on his console. The thing lit up with neon colors, and the radio turned on to a Bob Dylan song. He didn't understand most of the guy's lyrics, but he loved them. When a hint of vanilla wafted from the vents, Cassie rolled her eyes.

"Don't you dare." He figured she'd have a comment like she'd had about his Sperry's. He liked his Lexus, vanilla wafting and all. It beat the smells of himself after a day on set.

"Just go, Jake," Cassie demanded when he took too long.

The engine purred angrily as he put the car into gear. He raced to the ranch by memory. He'd driven every part of California and still got lost. Childhood roads were different. The paths were in him.

He glanced sideways at Cassie, who cracked her knuckles as she tapped her feet against the floor mat. They'd had a moment in front of the mirror, and he was going to kill this damn cow for ruining it. Then again, he'd told Cassie he was "just trying to get through this"—a lie because, even after all these years, she still left him wanting different things out of life; aching to change what could never be different.

Her knuckle-cracking sounded like small firecrackers.

He put his hand on her knee to calm her. Her skin was smooth and silky, like high threaded sheets. He reveled in it, sinking the pads of his fingers into her flesh. She let him.

"What are you doing?" Cassie swatted him away.

"Jesus Christ." He took his hand back and gripped his steering wheel with both fists. "I was trying to comfort you."

That was mostly true.

She stared out the window. "There's way too much irony in your sentence."

He grumbled at her dismissal, even as his groin needed a *down boy*. Her aggression was a strange aphrodisiac. He accelerated faster toward the ranch and pretended this was all a movie.

His old yard was in the same disarray as his thoughts as they pulled onto the property.

The city folks who Missy and Parker had invited for the weekend fled quicker than many of the Lovestruck locals, who pretended that intercepting a cow was no big deal as they subtly moved to their tents. The cow mooed from somewhere inside the barn.

"Don't park here," Cassie scolded. "You just ruined the yard tic-tac-toe, which was activity three on page four of Missy's packet."

"Really? Is our priority catching a cow or saving a yard game?"

"Fair point." Her breaths were heavy. "I just want

everything to be perfect for her."

"It will be." He wouldn't fault her for wanting everything to go as planned. He had the same goal, too.

"Thank you." She paused. "However, you still ruined the game."

Cassie jumped out of the Lexus, shouting over her shoulder, "I'm going to check on Sunny and Missy."

Was the woman ever going to go easy on him?

He growled with nobody around to hear it.

Then, he surveyed the situation.

Chaos.

Hysteria over a damn cow.

On instinct, he grabbed his dad's cowboy hat from the backseat. He put it on, got out of his car, and ran toward the barn where the family had once kept supplies. It was a round, not a square area—his father's pride and joy. The next round barn was hundreds of miles south of Lovestruck.

Two long tables were tipped over on his left. Dozens of chairs, each with burgundy bows, were legs up. A strand of white Christmas lights had been torn from the wall and were now hanging like icicles.

The cow was likely scared—rightfully so. She had interrupted Bridget Smith's daughter's wedding weekend.

"It's eating lettuce." A giggled voice startled him.

He glanced down to the little girl. Sunny. She pointed at the cow eating lettuce from a large salad bowl. Jake patted her head. The kid was cute even if she broke his heart a little. He recognized beyond any doubt she was Cassie's daughter as he stared at her. His gut wouldn't let him deny it this time.

"Your mom is looking for you."

She shrugged. "This is more fun."

Jake chuckled. He then focused on the issue at hand—the cow. Every time a man approached the animal, talking to her like a puppy, she charged toward one side of the barn and then the other, before grazing the bowl of food again.

Okay. The cow was hungry. *And* scared.

Several other men, his brother, Frankie, included, did some sort of jive around the animal. Jake was almost amused, if the cow wasn't dangerous. While Jake's idol was his rancher father, who'd taught him everything including how to wrangle an animal, Frankie's idol was whatever assholes inspired the *Wall Street* movies and the *Mad Men* television show. The oldest Smith male was no use in this context, beyond humor. He wore khaki shorts and a pink button-up shirt, his hair partially gelled back even though it was cropped short. Not that Jake blamed Frankie for being ill-prepared. He couldn't have predicted that catching a cow was part of his afternoon plans. Missy's guests were supposed to be playing volleyball, if he'd memorized the schedule correctly.

Still in his borrowed suit, Jake discarded the jacket and pulled his sleeves to his elbows. His knee was going to hurt but adrenaline pushed him forward. He'd already gotten through two bigger things this trip— seeing his mother and Cassie.

"I expected more from you, Frankie. That's not how you catch a cow," Jake reprimanded as he approached the action.

Frankie promptly stopped and threw up his hands. "Nice to see you, too."

Jake chuckled at his ability to still get under his

older brother's skin. In every other way, Frankie had him beat. A beautiful wife, or so he'd heard from Missy, and a steady, middleclass bank account, which didn't involve an aching body. Apparently, Frankie could also come back to Lovestruck without regret.

What was in Lovestruck for him all of a sudden?

He was likely just being the dutiful son everyone thought Jake would be.

Fucking props to Frankie.

Jake needed a horse. Now.

"Jake." Cassie's voice came from his left. She was fast-walking from the stable with a cocoa-colored horse and a lasso, as if reading his mind.

"Your sister's crying, but I've convinced her this is going to be a great story someday," Cassie said, picking up her stride.

She was a fantasy carrying reins and a lasso. She really was a cowgirl now.

He grabbed the items from her hand. "Good call."

Over his shoulder, he added, "thanks," as he guided the horse handily.

"I am capable of handling this, Jake. Come back here."

He doubted she could handle this, but even if she could, he didn't want her in harm's way. He was a gentleman. That was definitely the reason for his protectiveness. Definitely.

Jake mounted the horse easily and made sure Sunny was gone. The half-dozen men had aborted their mission. Only Frankie remained.

"Get out of the way," Jake shouted. To his astonishment, his brother listened.

With the lasso in his hand and the horse's reins in

the other, Jake lifted the rope and twirled it above his head. He struck a rhythm with the movement of his wrist, and when the rope was almost out of his control, he aimed and threw it over the cow's ears. He pulled hard after the rope fell around the cow's neck—at the right spot so he didn't hurt the animal. The cow struggled forcefully before the horse halted her.

His muscles were taut under his shirt as he tightened the rope around the cow so he could strengthen his hold.

Turning toward the barn door, he pulled the reins too harshly. Luckily, the horse ignored him.

Jake remained in control.

Sort of.

He gulped as Cassie bent to the ground, revealing her cleavage and then some. She picked up his hat a couple feet away. It must have fallen off during the cow wrangling. He was desperate to run his thumb down the visible line of her breasts and feel her heart against his palm.

He wanted their sweet summer romance back.

It was the first time he'd allowed a small crack of true longing to escape from his tough exterior. Although, this realization came because he'd seen Cassie's cleavage. He was officially a cave man. Man sees breasts. Man wants to touch them. Man wants to live with them forever.

Cassie was a mirage as she dusted off the hat and walked toward him. She stared at the rim like she was admiring something precious. Maybe she wished to go back, too. Maybe their small play at teamwork reminded her of their friendship. Maybe she'd suspended her disdain for his Sperry's because he could still pull off a cowboy hat.

He closed his eyes for several seconds to keep his emotions where they belonged—out of view. When he reached for his hat, Cassie backed away in playful jest.

He nearly fell off the horse.

"Dammit, Cassie."

"I'm sorry." She held out the hat.

He placed it on his head before turning his attention to walking the cow to her proper pasture. She'd stopped fighting and was eating off the ground, piles of cake, which he guessed had been tonight's dessert.

"I could've lassoed the cow by myself," Cassie mumbled. She couldn't take it easy on him. She was still stubborn as hell.

"I know you could've." He still didn't know if she could have, but the icy stare she gave him was enough to keep him from debating it. Maybe Cassie had learned to lasso, like she'd learned to run a dude ranch while looking like an absolute knockout. Why had she decided to turn the family ranch into a dude ranch? She was a city girl.

"But thank you, Jake. For helping."

He nodded. "You're welcome."

He signaled the horse to move and trotted out of the barn.

"Tell Missy it'll be fine. If dinner is ruined, we'll order pizzas," he called to his mom, who was on the phone and sitting on the front porch, fanning herself with one of her beloved romance novels. He'd learned how to kiss from his mom's novel collection—a secret he'd go to his grave with if he could help it.

His mom's voice was firm but kind from a

distance. "I love you, dearly, Pearl, but you're going to have to make this up to my baby girl."

She must've been explaining to Mr. Karl's wife what had happened at the ranch. Jake would hate to be Pearl right now. That was saying something, given he could barely stand himself.

"Mom's a good woman," he said under his breath. When he'd talked to her last night, she'd spared him any tough questions, maybe not to spook him. She'd let him sit at her table, like when they'd separate peas from their pods together years ago. Sure, it hadn't been the warmest of welcomes, but she hadn't kicked his ass, either.

"Bridget's the best," Cassie answered.

He jumped.

Cassie had followed him toward Mr. Karl's place. He glanced over his shoulder several times. She walked, head down, avoiding his stare. She moved as if she was on a tight rope—like a misstep might send her into a pack of lions.

"Is something wrong?"

She shook her head.

"You sure?" He didn't probe because he wanted the answer, but because he couldn't help himself. He still gave a damn about what was going on in that head of hers.

Cassie shrugged.

He shook his head at how stubborn she was. "Are you scared I'll run off again? Because I wouldn't do that to Missy."

Cassie's gaze met his.

"And what about me?" Her words stammered out of her.

"It's best you turn around now if you want to talk about that history."

"Of course. You never talk about anything. I'd be nice to clear the air before the wedding. At least a little."

He turned, stopping both animals, and Cassie, in their tracks. "I think seven years away speaks plenty."

She blew hair from her forehead. "You're such an ass."

"Bet you've been waiting a long time to get those words out," he mumbled.

"Yeah that, and you're a coward."

Jake matched his breathing with the trotting of the horse's hooves. "Then why don't you go away?"

He meant it.

"Go," he repeated.

His chest hurt. The reason he'd left Lovestruck seven years ago didn't add up anymore. Back then, he'd wanted to tell her how lost he was, but he didn't know how to explain it without sounding like a weak man. She'd met him as a cowboy-in-training. Strong. Invincible. Cassie had been distant those dark days when he was falling apart. He'd blamed his own shift in behavior for her reaction. Plus, she'd been dealing with her parents' shit, along with helping Missy mourn their dad. She hadn't needed to witness his vulnerability on top of it. He'd been no good for her after his dad died. He'd been no good for anyone.

"I'm not leaving. You have my horse," Cassie answered, as if her words were a reasonable excuse.

"I'll return it."

"I'm very protective of my horses, especially Caramel, so I'll bring him back myself."

"You named this animal Caramel?"

The horse neighed lightly, as if to say, *shut the hell up, I like my name.*

Cassie reiterated the sentiment in English. Jake, Cassie, and Caramel stayed quiet as they jogged along, listening to the breeze through the long prairie grass. It sounded like the ocean, which he lived near-*ish* to in California. He didn't miss water like he missed the hills of the Smith property. He liked land more than anything. Solid ground. Cassie's eyes.

"My daughter named him Caramel."

He pulled on the horse's reins. "Sunny."

"Yes. Sunny's my baby."

"She looks just like you," he admitted. A chill spread across his shoulders—a sharp tightness. He'd suspected. *Damn.* He'd known since last night that Sunny was hers, but the confirmation still tore through him like a gust of wind chilling his bones.

The little girl wasn't his; he and Cassie had always used protection together. He couldn't reconcile if it calmed him or riled him that she'd moved on quickly after he'd left. Everything within him was heavy. But like most things in life, it was what it was. Life consisted of accepting the bad and living with it, no matter the bruises. The good times were sweeteners to keep a man or woman moving.

"What's her real name?"

"Sunny is her real name. She was smiling the minute she came out of me." Cassie grinned at the memory. Her emotion—evident and beautiful—destroyed him.

Fuck.

He'd once thought they'd share that rite of

passage—parenthood—together. He had, at one point, been part of the story she went on to create with someone else.

Her confirmation was a hornet's bite to his ass.

"*Sunny*brook Inn and Dude Ranch. I get the name now."

For the next several moments, the only sounds, once again came from walking hooves and swaying prairie grass on either side of the horse trail Cassie must've added to the property. Pride stopped him from admitting the needed addition was a good one.

She bit her bottom lip. "I saw the latest movie you were in. Did you really jump off a motorcycle?"

"You watched me?" He ignored her second question.

She shrugged. "You've got a couple of fans in Lovestruck who've kept up with you."

"You and Mom?" He recalled his conversation with his mom last night.

"I love going with Bridget. She enjoys watching her son in the pictures. It's borderline embarrassing how excited she gets to see you. Popcorn flies everywhere."

Cassie walked faster so she was next to him and the horse instead of behind them. "You could get really hurt doing those tricks."

He answered with a clipped, "Yeah."

Physical pain had nothing on other pain. This weekend was already reminding him. Still, the month leading up to his arrival in Lovestruck was far worse than the reality had been so far. The sleepless nights wondering what Cassie would look like or if she'd even acknowledge him.

"Were you limping at the boutique earlier?"

"I reckon." He was less than graceful these days. He worked his body hard and no longer in the ways he wanted to. A groan escaped him as images of making love to Cassie all those years ago crept up. She hadn't been his first partner, but everything about intimacy had felt different when they were together—like they were opposite sides of the same coin.

"You should take care of yourself, Jake."

"Let it alone now," he answered. "You sound like my little missus, worrying."

"Did you just say that? Can you respect me enough to not go there, cowboy? That *is* way too in the past."

"Fine." He guided the cow back to her side of the grassland. She was more than willing to go peacefully once the lasso was removed. Mr. Karl was already mending the broken fence.

"I heard what happened. I sure am sorry," he said. "Tell Missy I'll make it up to her. Pearl is working on food for the big dinner tonight."

"Luckily, no one got hurt." Jake hopped off the horse.

Rip.

"Dammit."

Cassie turned from her kinder pleasantries with Mr. Karl, rubbing her crossed arms though it wasn't cold outside. "What was that?"

He tilted his head, straining to glimpse at his ass.

"Did you rip your pants, Jake?"

Yep. He had ripped his pants.

Chapter Five

Cassie

Cassie squinted in the direction of Jake's backside. "Are you sure?"

Karma was her friend if his pants had ripped. He deserved a good tear in the trousers. A good kick in the pants, too.

"What other kind of rip do you think it was?" He added, "Don't answer that."

Jake was a little too upset about the incident, cursing like he was in real trouble.

She laughed into her hand cupped over her mouth. "Easy there, cowboy. They're pants."

"They're *the* pants, remember? I'm supposed to wear them to the wedding tomorrow. I can't very well walk my sister down the aisle with my ass hanging out."

"Oh." *Oh.*

Missy had chosen Jake to walk her down the aisle? Maybe she didn't want her brother running off again and the important role minimized those chances. Cassie's second thought was more selfish.

Why can't Jake walk with his backside hanging out?

She didn't like the question, especially after Jake had scolded her for still caring about him by asking questions a wife would ask, apparently. She wouldn't know what questions a wife would ask. She'd never gotten married. She'd gotten close once after Jake left town. Thank God, she hadn't gone through with it. Cassie was a single mother for practically four years before Sunny's father more consistently re-entered the picture. That is, after he'd established himself as a big-city professional.

It'd been an evolving journey toward normalcy since then.

Now Jake was messing with it. He was messing with everything.

"I see your point," she muttered. Although, she could think of worse things to set her eyes on than Jake's behind, even despite her hating him at the moment. His ass in pants was the only reason she hadn't hurt him when he'd refused to talk to her a couple minutes ago. She'd looked at his backside as they'd made their way to the Karl property—a fun game he had no idea she was playing.

Given the cow fiasco today, she was certain Missy wouldn't find the humor in this "ripped pants" mishap. When the cow was loose, Cassie had found her friend sobbing in one of the inn's bathrooms. She'd soothed Missy and told her it would be okay. Cassie had learned that after a disaster, life would be okay again. Maybe a little dimmer in some way, but it still moved forward. Heartbreak meant something. There was a certain amount of courage in it.

She and Jake exchanged glances. She sighed despite herself at how handsome he was every damn time she looked at him. Jake embodied the truest form of romantic love she'd ever known. If she could keep their memories in that light, she wasn't so irritated at him. He was family. He really was family, even if he didn't know it. Even if he left Lovestruck after this weekend without learning the facts about anything other than her ability to lasso.

She knew how to do a lot of things.

Run a dude ranch.

Be a mother.

Give up dreams.

Keep a secret.

Cassie took Caramel's reins, said good-bye to Mr. Karl, and turned toward Jake. He was still glancing behind him, mumbling curses.

She rolled her eyes. "I will mend your pants when I tailor them tonight. The harder part is going to be steaming the horse stink out of your shirt."

She would add these tasks to her "to do" list.

There was an early season summer camp arriving at the beginning of next week, and she had no idea where she'd find the time to change the ranch back into a functioning dude ranch in such a short time after the wedding. However, she needed the business.

Jake followed her quietly toward and into the stable. Their silence wasn't awkward, but she didn't like how it made her almost blurt out everything.

All that had happened in seven years.

She took a brush and worked on Caramel's mane.

Behind her, she heard Jake rustle with a button-up shirt and a pair of coveralls from the hook near the lassos. She stored extra work clothes in the barn, so she didn't traipse the smell of barn animals into her home.

"A little extravagant, don't you think?"

Cassie glanced over her shoulder and gulped as he

buttoned up his shirt. She didn't need to witness the perfection of his pecs. Sure, she wanted to stare at his broad chest with the perfect amount of hair showcased, but she didn't *need* to see it. The small glimpse of him she drank in would be in her dreams for weeks. He was too hot for his own good.

"Missy and Parker are riding out on Caramel tomorrow at sunset. This horse has to look perfect."

Jake turned toward her, liquid splashing from the bucket in his hand. He'd busied himself replenishing water in each stall after he'd changed his clothing. Once a cowboy, always a cowboy. She wished the sentiment was true. With Matthew Smith's cowboy hat on his head and the want to save the day in his heart, she recognized Jake again today. She more than recognized him. She wanted him. The murky part of herself who made bad decisions spoke to her in a whisper—*He's still everything to you.*

Unfortunately, the murky part of herself was also stupid and unaware of logic. Jake wasn't in love with her anymore. He was here for one specific purpose: his sister. He'd made that clear, no matter any progress in being civil toward her.

"You've got to be kidding me." Jake chuckled.

She stared blankly at him.

"They're riding out on a horse?" he said. "Like Cinderella?"

"What's so wrong with your baby sister wanting a fairy-tale day?" She continued brushing Caramel's hair. It was mostly smooth now, shiny against the sun coming in from the open stable doors. The animal looked otherworldly—majestic even—and she wished she believed in fairy-tales. In a way she did. Watching life through Sunny's eyes gave her faith that fairies were real and life could be lived with hope. She needed hope as she struggled to not only keep the dude ranch afloat but to keep the land in her name.

She believed her reasoning still held true—Jake would want it someday.

"Nothing's wrong with wanting a fairy-tale day so long as she understands there's no such thing as a fairy-tale life. This marriage will be horseshit—pardon my pun, Caramel—if that's the foundation they're building on."

"You don't think your sister understands, Jake?" She put her hands on her hips. "After all your family's been through."

He had the good sense to keep quiet.

"Don't let our love story make you such a sourpuss."

"We weren't much of a story, Cassie. Four months of passion. That's a drop in the bucket."

"Really?" Tears filled her eyes. She lowered her head and sniffled. She needed to breathe. She hadn't cried over Jake in years, and she wouldn't crack in front of him, especially since he had a gigantic chip on his shoulder that wasn't melting fast enough. Having a breakdown in front of him would to be a whole other level of embarrassing. Demoralizing. Unacceptable.

"What's wrong?" he asked.

"Allergies."

"Bullshit." He stared at the high-beamed ceiling and growled. "Cass, I didn't mean to say it that way."

"How did you mean to say it then, Tin Man?" Her icy stare locked with his when he looked at her again.

"We were happy, weren't we?" She'd been waiting

to ask the question for years. People who were happy didn't run away like Jake had. But people who were unhappy also didn't smile the way she had when she was with him. Her take on their relationship was obviously the wrong one. *No* was the most logical answer. She needed to hear it from him. Then, she could tell him the truth about what happened—about how Sunny happened.

He took his hat off and stared at it. "Yes."

"Yes?" she seethed.

"Yes," he repeated, nearly spitting the word out. "We were happy."

"What kind of answer is that?" His response was supposed to match his departure from her life. It was supposed to be *no*. *No* made sense.

"It's the answer you wanted. Can't that be enough right now? Will I ever be enough?"

Her eyes widened, and her lips parted.

"It," he corrected. His chest heaved, and he shook his head. "Will *it* ever be enough?"

"You didn't feel good enough for me?"

He glanced away.

"Jake, you were everything." The brush dropped from her hand, making a loud and echoed thud.

Jake filled the last tub of water before he set down the bucket and plodded out of the stable.

She followed him toward his tent. "We're not done."

"Let's not air our dirty laundry around people." He opened the flap door.

"Why not? Everyone already gossips about us," she argued, though she did lower her voice.

He slammed the tent flap behind him. The lack of

noise was almost funny. Almost.

Jake was such a dick.

She wanted to tell him to mend his own pants, but that would only hurt Missy, so she settled for giving him a scoff resembling Caramel's annoyed shudder.

"Please help me, Matthew Smith." She prayed to Jake's dad. "I don't want to kick your son in the behind. Jake. I'm talking about Jake." She clarified which Smith son was causing her trouble this time. Her heart beats quickened, and she soothed them with the fact Jake couldn't disappear again. He still had a wedding to attend. For at least thirty-some more hours, she'd know where he was and how to find him. Why did that make her feel safe? It shouldn't have. Jake, of anyone, proved how much people could surprise her; disappoint her; hurt her.

For now, she needed to move on with her day.

"See you later, cowboy." Cassie turned.

A hand gripped her wrist and pulled her backward. She stumbled into the tent, stopping against a hard torso. Jake was as sturdy as a wall.

He turned her to face him, and she didn't have time to say or do anything. Instead, she reacted with a gurgled sigh as his lips met her pursed ones. It didn't matter what her brain thought of this kiss—it would have its say eventually. Her body had wanted Jake since the bridal boutique, and it was speaking louder than anything else.

Jake's fists gripped the fabric over her ribcage and her backside as he pulled her harder against him.

She brushed her hands up his sides and wrapped her arms around his neck. Her fingers fisted his hair, and she sighed like she'd been given a piece of chocolate after days of no sugar.

His body was hard.

Every part.

He smelled like fields and woody cologne.

Her heart sped as the world slowed. She wasn't a mother; a dude ranch owner; an amateur designer; Jake's ex. She was a woman wanted. Her hands dropped from his hair to his shoulders, down his arms as sturdy as tree stumps. She'd never experience nature the same way again.

"You're like a sculpture," she mumbled as his lips kissed her jawline, trailing down her neck. She stared at the ceiling of the tent, and her mind returned to her with an annoying vengeance, despite how good his mouth tended to every inch of flesh he touched along her collarbone.

She had unfinished business, but this kiss affected more than just her and Jake. There was Sunny to remember. And Sunny's father. And Missy. And Bridget. And a lot of people were in this tent. She refused to behave like her mother who had no inclination to protect her family when she'd had her affair. The humiliation was more than Cassie could endure healthily at a young age. Her mother's actions changed the course of Cassie's life. It led her to Lovestruck. To this moment, which she filled with her own mistakes.

"Jake." She pressed her palms against his chest and pushed him away, needing life to move forward not backward.

"Cassie." He protested but listened, hands up in surrender.

They couldn't kiss and expect seven years of

estrangement to go away. Gosh, it would be nice if mouth-to-mouth recitation worked in this instance.

She gazed around the tent to keep from admitting how much she enjoyed their make-out session. How, if pushed even a little more, she'd give into something that would complicate an already complicated situation.

Not only was Jake leaving in a couple days, but he had no idea why she had never reached out to him more than once when he'd fled in the first place. Jake didn't know the years between *that* moment and this one. He had no idea she'd almost gotten married shortly after he left, and she'd spent much of her time atoning for the choice to keep her daughter. She gave up everything— her budding fashion dream and an easier life. She'd told Sunny's father the truth so he had the opportunity to step up, even if it would cause a lifetime of trouble for the Smith family. Every decision she'd made pushed her away from what she'd wanted—what she still wanted on her weakest days.

Jake + Cassie.

If those names were a carving in an old desk that didn't make sense anymore, then why did she still keep it so she could look at it every day?

This moment proved she was a fool.

"Cassie."

"I need to be the one who runs away this time," she whispered.

Before he could answer, she fled. And the thing that broke her heart all over again was he didn't run after her. He let her go.

He was too good at letting her go.

Chapter Six

Cassie

Missy was in her childhood room when Cassie found her. The space had been converted to a guest room, but there were still parts with Missy's touch—the frilly, ivory curtains; the lavender paint color; and, the vanity, which Matthew Smith had carved for his baby girl. Missy had left the piece when she moved out of the house because it felt like a part of the home. The ranch house, now the inn, was filled with these treasures.

Cassie wasn't sentimental about material things, but this place was an exception. Everything in it had a connection to something or someone who meant a lot to the Smith family.

Her chest tightened at the reality she may not be able to retain it much longer. The bills were piling up quicker than she could pay them, evidence the dude ranch was struggling after a more developed dude ranch popped up two towns over. It had a Ferris wheel, and a claim to fame. She couldn't compete, no matter how wonderful her returning guests and camps were.

She'd learned from her mom's political career about loyalty—a tricky notion for most people. The shiny, sparkly promise of something new spoke more powerfully than tradition. No one was to blame. She only had so much to offer. Quaint and cute and homey

56

was her vision for this place, along with teaching kids what ranching was like without making a mockery of it.

She blew out a breath.

Her professional woes weren't important this weekend.

She had bigger issues.

"The pizzas are ordered, and people are back on track with the fun." Cassie knocked on the doorframe, so she didn't startle Missy. Parker sat on the quilt comforter-covered bed with his fiancée. Both were scribing in separate notebooks. "Your mother's cousins are working on salvaging the barn. The cupcakes were already setting out when the cow trampled in, but no worries, we're on it."

"The cupcakes were ruined, too?" Missy looked up, her expression dropping. "The ones we paid hundreds of dollars to ship from Philly?"

The request was outlandish, but even the most laidback brides tended to outdo themselves when their wedding day was involved.

Bridget must have fibbed to Missy when she'd explained there was minimal damage this morning. Cassie didn't need the Smith matriarch getting into trouble for the strings they had to pull—sending fresh eggs for six months—in order to bribe the bakery to share their secret recipes. Her staff was recreating the treats.

"It's all good," she said, moving the conversation along with, "What are you two lovebirds doing?"

"We're working on our vows." Missy looked back at her paper and slowly began scribbling again.

"Next to each other?" That seemed as taboo as the groom seeing the bride on the wedding day.

Parker pushed his thick-rimmed, black glasses up the bridge of his nose. He was a doctor in Boston, and he looked the part—chiseled and well-groomed. He was a thinner Clark Kent. There was no way this guy was going to be mounting a horse and whisking Missy away in a smooth manner. He was all urban with the heart of a country boy. Cassie would have to bring the step stool and a first-aid kit to the reception.

"No laptop?" she asked.

Parker shrugged. "Missy wants us to do this the old-fashioned way. I've had my vows typed for months. I'm copying everything down by hand because it's 'romantic.' My handwriting looks like chicken scratch."

"Your chicken scratch *is* more romantic." Missy nearly stabbed through her paper as she wrote her last punctuation on the page. "All done. I won't get through these words without crying."

She glanced at Cassie again. "I want everything to be as magical as possible. It's the one day in a person's life when it can be."

Parker kissed her forehead and stood, tucking his notes into his pants pocket. "It will be. I promise. I'm going to partake in a game of Frisbee with my groomsmen. See you later, sweetheart."

He apparently knew the unwritten rule of girl talk. No boys were allowed during it.

Missy smiled as he left the room.

"I see you looking at his behind." Cassie folded her arms over her chest, quirking an eyebrow.

"I'm sure you've gotten a good look at a certain guy's behind yourself. I heard Jake did quite the job catching Mr. Karl's cow."

Cassie hadn't come upstairs to talk about Jake,

although he was still on her mind. Either way, she wouldn't mention he'd been wearing his wedding pants while playing cowboy hero. This conversation would turn sour quickly if she did.

"I've caught a couple glimpses."

"What's wrong then?" Missy asked.

Cassie cringed. How was it that her friend always knew when something was on her mind?

She slumped onto the bed. "It's nothing. You should go downstairs and enjoy your guests."

Missy side-hugged her. "I haven't seen you in a couple months."

True. Missy and Parker lived so far away and much of the wedding planning had been done over the phone and email.

"I've been off recently." Cassie stood and redid her hair into a high bun. As she stared into the mirror over the vanity, Missy read her vows quietly, smiling at places.

Cassie wanted to hear them, but it would've been out of obligation. Listening to Missy praise her love story and talk about forever wasn't the healthiest idea. She adored that Missy was happy, but she wished to be happier in her own love life.

Clarification: She simply wanted a love life.

"Seriously, how's it going with Jake?" Missy interrupted her pity party thoughts.

That was about as loaded a question as a baked potato with all the toppings, and Cassie didn't want to answer. This was Missy and Parker's wedding weekend.

She turned, supporting herself against the vanity. Flashbacks of times she and Missy would talk about boys and life and dreams filled the space. Missy had done most of the talking back then because Cassie had felt weird gushing over Jake Smith. A little sister was mostly uninterested in how good her older brother was at seducing his girlfriend. Plus, she and Jake had the kind of love that people made gag motions at; the kind that made people warn, "Be careful. You're going to burn out."

Their kiss in the tent today proved something in both of them hadn't burnt out yet. And God, it was good. It was so good.

"We're getting along as well as can be expected," Cassie answered. "It's just—" She rolled her eyes. "He's so annoying."

She was relieved to get those words off her chest. It was the least dangerous truth.

Missy laughed. "And stubborn."

"And headstrong."

"And guarded," Missy answered. "He won't say more than two words to me when we pass each other. They're always nice words, but still. He's so broody."

"And hot." Cassie sighed.

"Gross." Missy threw a pillow at Cassie's face, and they laughed. When their voices settled, Missy added, "At least he's being civil, given the circumstances. It's not every day you see your ex again, and she has a child, who, by the way was fathered by—"

"He doesn't know," Cassie interrupted, shaking her head.

Missy stared. "Know what?"

Cassie's head hadn't stopped shaking, so Missy shook her head, too. "Why are we still doing this?"

"He never knew I was pregnant, let alone whose

child Sunny is."

"What?"

Cassie stopped shaking her head and stood motionless.

"I had reasons," she said, blurting out her excuses. At first, she had figured Jake would come back, and she'd tell him in person the mess she'd gotten into. Then, he didn't come back, and her heart broke as her anger toward him deepened. He'd abandoned her for no apparent reason. After Sunny was born, her world changed entirely. She had needed to figure her life out, and Jake would have complicated any foot forward in that pursuit. Eventually, too much time had passed and telling Jake had seemed frivolous. He hadn't bothered keeping in touch with the family, except for his mother on holidays—and he kept the calls short.

"See what I'm saying?" Cassie finished. She waited for her best friend to affirm she wasn't a terrible person. Hadn't she built a solid case?

Missy paced the room, rubbing her forehead. "Cheese and rice," she muttered, stopping mid-stride and staring at Cassie. "Oh. My. God. You never told Jake you got pregnant by his brother? What? *What?* Shit almighty."

Missy never swore. Cassie opened her mouth to speak but was interrupted.

"This is fucked-up. I mean, it was always fucked-up, but this—" Missy stared at the floor. "This is fucked up."

And there she went meeting her curse quota for four years.

"I tried to go to California and tell him. A year after I had Sunny, and Jake hadn't come back."

"What happened?" Missy asked.

"I chickened out when I went, and the number I got was his agent's, who basically hung up on me after telling me Jake was on a date at his movie premiere."

"Why would that matter?" Missy asked. "You weren't looking for—"

Cassie bit her bottom lip as tears broke from her eyes.

"Oh." Missy covered her mouth. "You hadn't given up on him. Not really. But Cass, how could you hold onto hope for Jake when Frankie's Sunny's dad?"

"I don't know," she confessed. She covered her face with her hands and growled. "It was one stupid night with Frankie. It messed up everything. I can't even say I regret it though, because I love my daughter."

"Both things can be true," Missy said.

"This scenario is something out of Greek mythology," Cassie mumbled.

She'd relayed what had happened between Frankie and her an uncomfortable amount of times with Bridget. She'd met the oldest Smith brother at Lushes on Main Street. She and Frankie had gone into their four minutes of passion, in the very romantic bathroom stall, knowing what it was—a one-night stand. They weren't supposed to mean anything to each other. She hadn't known Frankie was Jake's older brother until he had his farewell dinner at the Smith home the next night—also the night she'd met Jake. She also hadn't known that hers and Frankie's pact to keep their broken condom fiasco a secret would be exposed because of her pregnancy. Life had a cruel sense of humor.

"Holy crap, Cassie," Missy repeated.

"I'm so sorry. I don't want to spoil this weekend." Cassie forced a smirk. "Forget I said anything."

"I can't un-hear this. Jake really doesn't know?"

"I was hoping he would be less angry, so I could tell him. We're still in a fight I can't pinpoint the exact beginning to. I don't know how to tell him at this point. Or if it's even necessary."

Missy stood and walked toward her. "Of course, it's necessary. I'd hoped this weekend would be the start of Jake visiting Mom in Lovestruck and me out in Boston. I mean, it took a lot of phone calls to get him to answer. But his response means something. I know my brother. He misses us."

Missy paused, nodding as if figuring something out in her head. "If Jake hasn't avoided us because of your pregnancy, then he probably feels like a big old dummy for not knowing how to come home. Or maybe he doesn't know how to feel about you. Maybe he always sensed a secret. Maybe we don't know that he knew you had a child."

"If he did know about Sunny, he didn't show it when they met last night," Cassie said.

"They did?"

"It was adorable and brief." She sighed. "And I told him she was my daughter today. I don't know, Missy. I prefer to think he's just a dumbass."

"Why did Jake leave Lovestruck? I can't figure it out."

Cassie bit her lip to keep it from trembling. "It was a really devastating time. I don't remember much, honestly."

Missy's forehead scrunched. "You're right. I hardly recall those couple months after Dad died, and you lied at first about why you didn't return to school with me."

"I didn't exactly lie when I said I hadn't wanted to face my mother. It just wasn't my mother's affair I was worried about anymore."

Missy inhaled. "And my mom was struggling with the loss of Dad. I know this sounds awful, but I was happy you got pregnant and ended up with her in town. Once you told me the real reason you stayed, that is."

It was Cassie's turn to throw the pillow. She walked over to the bed and found the fluffiest one to toss at her friend—her sister from another mister.

"Gee, thanks," she added as the pillow hit Missy's shoulder.

"I mean it in a good way, Cassie. Mom loves babies, and your parents weren't around. I think it was perfect for you two to have each other."

She agreed. In many ways, Bridget had saved her life. She'd done the three a.m. feedings with her; taught her how to help Sunny latch. Bridget had slept next to Cassie the first year of Sunny's life as Cassie dealt with being abandoned by her family, by Frankie, as he continued his career path out-of-state, and by Jake. The Smith matriarch had taught her how to be a good mom by being a good mom.

"My dad tried," Cassie said. "He was heartbroken over my mother, and he didn't know how to be there for me. Plus, he didn't want people writing anything in the paper or online. It truly was a 'you can't go home again' situation." She paused. "Maybe that's what Jake was going through after he left. But why couldn't he come home?"

They'd arrived back to that question. Why had Jake

left?

"Do you think you could wait until after my wedding to ask him? And to tell him any of this crap?" Missy asked. Tears filled her eyes as she took her time to continue. "I know it's selfish, but this is all too much."

"It's not selfish. You deserve your day."

Missy rubbed the bridge of her nose. "The thing is, Dad's not here, and Jake's so much like Dad. I really want him to be the one to walk me down the aisle."

Cassie cleared her throat. Missy had picked Jake for a more profoundly intimate reason than she'd imagined. Jake did resemble Matthew Smith in demeanor. Her reason to choose him for the important role made sense now.

Missy was right.

Her conversation with Jake had to wait until after the wedding. There were too many reasons for him to run again if he found out the truth sooner.

But what if he left before she could say anything?

Besides that, their shared kiss in his tent complicated matters, didn't it? Cassie would have to avoid Jake without appearing like she was avoiding him.

They'd made out.

It was fantastic.

She'd have to stop the story there.

Hypocrite.

She'd been badgering Jake an hour ago about opening up, and now she was quitting him cold turkey. Maybe not cold turkey, but she had to at least act unaffected by him.

"I won't say anything until after your wedding,"

she promised. She turned toward the mirror again. "Do you think there's a chance Jake never loved me?"

Tears flooded her eyes.

"Why would you ask that?" Missy gently gripped her shoulder.

"He was always the romantic one, Missy. The guy who could look out at the vast horizon at the edge of this property and not be frightened by it. Jake used to believe in me, and then he left, and I thought I had worked through that rejection." She shook her head, and teardrops marched down her cheek like sad little soldiers. "Why does this still hurt?"

It was strange the way some wounds only scabbed over in life but never truly healed. They simply mended enough so a person could put one foot in front of the other and call it resilience.

Cassie looked toward the ceiling and mumbled, "He didn't care as much as I did."

"That can't be true," Missy responded. But she didn't say anything else.

Chapter Seven

Jake

Jake rubbed the bridge of his nose. He was tired of looking at pictures of himself.

As a toddler.

And a school kid.

And a teenager.

He wanted to be back in the tent with Cassie. He wasn't so mad about his sleeping accommodations anymore. It had been sexy hearing the commotion of Missy and Parker's guests playing field games while he'd made out with Cassie for the first, and probably the last, time in years.

He craved kissing her again even while he'd been kissing her. Then she'd run off before they'd resolved anything beyond proving they were still attracted to each other. It was more than physical attraction for him, but how much more? His feelings were muddled. He'd had a whiplash of emotions in twenty-four hours. A one-man rodeo.

He'd followed Cassie out of the tent, though she hadn't noticed. He'd fallen behind when a couple of neighbors stopped to talk to him. Parker had then found him halfway up the ranch house's stairs and led him back to the first floor, saying something about Missy and Cassie needing "girl time." Jake was lassoed into a

Frisbee game with the guys instead.

He now sat next to his mother at the kitchen table, while a herd of women prepared cupcakes behind them. The helpers had arrived shortly after the cow got to her proper pasture and after the suckers who failed to wrangle said cow had begun cleaning up the barn. They were much better at that task.

Frankie with a broom was a sight.

Outside, games were still underway, and the high octaves of cheering gave Jake an extra special headache. His mom had ordered pizzas from the local pie shop to compensate for the food lost earlier. They'd have an eclectic display for dinner, and Missy was now convinced it was better than Plan A.

"All is good in Missy's world." His mom smiled, telling him everything.

So Cassie hadn't need to get her panties in a bunch. The day had been salvaged.

Cassie's panties. In a bunch. Preferably in his tent.

Those were great but misplaced thoughts. He shook his head, discarding another picture from an album that wouldn't make for a good centerpiece. Missy had purchased dozens of antique frames to put the images in. He was perverse for thinking about Cassie's underwear while sitting next to his mother and looking at photos, especially when he was already worked up.

Cassie had kissed him the same way she used to— only every touch and peck was better because he'd savored it—knowing this time around, it wasn't guaranteed to happen again. Kissing her was a privilege. And now white lace panties were in the forefront of his damn thoughts. His goal hadn't been to see them when his lips touched hers. It wasn't his ultimate goal anyway.

He'd been frustrated at her—angry that she'd publicly demanded an explanation from him. His frustration awakened his need to touch her in hopes she would reciprocate. She had definitely reciprocated. But there was shit they had to trudge through before kissing again. He didn't have big enough boots to do it. Not only that, but he'd purposefully built a life far away from Lovestruck, and that life had him on his way to another job in a couple of days. His joints ached at the thought already.

But he liked his life. He did.

"What about this one?" His mom nudged his arm, handing Jake a picture of him and Frankie in the tub, dumping water on a two-year-old Missy. Her gaping mouth and closed-eyed toddler face revealed she was already sick of her brothers.

The image was a perfect moment to share, except—"My pecker's out." Jake flicked the picture into the "no" pile.

Frankie walked into the kitchen with a beer in one hand. He snatched the photo with the other. "You haven't grown much, have you, Jake."

He clearly needed to get payback for Jake's team beating his at Frisbee.

"I'm man enough to catch a wild animal, which is more than I can say about you."

"It was a cow," Frankie said flatly.

"And you were scared."

"Boys, honest to Pete," their mom muttered, not taking her eyes from another picture in her grip. "Could you please try to act your ages?" She sighed. "And you're right, Jake. We don't want your willy showing in any of these pictures."

"Willy" was as close to a dirty word as his mom ever used. Unless "honest to Pete" counted, too.

Frankie sat down across from him, turning one of the leather-bound photo albums toward himself. "I'm sorry."

His brother's easy retreat pissed him off even more. Jake bit his tongue. The fact was, he didn't know why he and his brother were at odds with one another. They hadn't always been a shitshow. But since they were teens, Jake picked fights. Frankie annoyed the hell out of him, maybe because he played second fiddle around his brother, as if his dreams to own the family ranching business weren't big enough. When Jake fled Lovestruck, he'd discovered Frankie was right. It was good to explore his options. There was a big world out there and people who accepted him as someone other than a rancher.

"Done with the yard games?" He hoped Frankie only needed a beer break. His brother was too comfortable on his ass across from him.

"Nah, I came in because Missy's looking for Mom. Plus, it's hot as hell out there."

It wasn't "hot as hell," but Frankie could barely handle temperatures above seventy-two degrees. He'd been useless in the fields as a young man.

"Well, you found her."

Frankie chuckled.

Jake hated his brother's flippancy. He preferred a good physical showdown. This bickering like old hens was more irritating. Frankie's wife, whom he had yet to meet, must've been the reason for his softened attitude.

She was surely a saint.

After all, someone or something guided his brother toward becoming a hometown man.

"Sunny's having a ball out there," Cassie muttered, entering the kitchen.

"She's getting so big," Frankie said. "I haven't seen her since Mother's Day, and I swear she's grown three inches."

"Yeah," Cassie answered. "Kids grow quickly. You only get them once at these precious ages."

Jake didn't miss the emphasis in her tone, like she was scolding everyone for not valuing time or life or each other. She was right.

The room quieted.

Jake glanced between Frankie and Cassie. They'd developed a friendship. He guessed since Frankie started visiting more often. Made sense with Cassie practically part of the Smith family.

"You're a good woman, Cassandra," Frankie finally answered.

She set a bowl of red grapes in the middle of the table. Her chest was inches from Jake's face. He didn't glance toward her or acknowledge the soft brush of her arm against his as she straightened. His hair stood on his forearms, and he adjusted himself in his seat. The wooden bench beneath him creaked. He popped a grape into his mouth and had a full-on coughing fit.

"Allergic to pretty girls, Jake?" Frankie asked. "Cassie's surely better than any woman you've come across since her."

Cassie muttered something under her breath that sounded like, "Help me, Lord."

"Don't sell yourself short," Frankie answered.

Jake shook his head. He didn't need to explain the relationships he'd had since Cassie. She'd been respectful not to parade anyone around. Besides, there wasn't much to say on his end. He ignored the tinge of jealousy he had toward Frankie being such a damn gentleman, touting Cassie's praises. His brother wasn't trying to charm her. Frankie was married, for Christ's sake. Which meant, he was being a dick on purpose. Figured.

"I don't have enough time to woo women."

"Jake deserves to have a life, Frankie," Cassie said.

Jake relaxed at her words. It was the closest thing to forgiveness he'd receive from her. She moved around the edge of the table, broom in hand. He hadn't noticed she had it under her arm when she'd set down the grapes. She busied herself tidying up.

"If he's had or has a girlfriend or fiancée, it's his business."

Had she said it because she had a boyfriend or fiancé and wanted approval? Or was she being genuinely okay if he'd moved on? They'd kissed, and Cassie wouldn't allow him to touch her if she was serious with another guy. Still, she avoided eye contact with him.

"I don't have anyone." He didn't want her to think their kiss earlier was anything other than giving into his want to do so. "I work a lot, and I enjoy that. I'm alone at night."

Those were the facts.

"Me, too." She turned toward him, biting the corner of her bottom lip.

His mom had looked up somewhere during the conversation, and now it was too weird to continue. The bird clock on the wall chirped.

Jake had always hated that damn thing.

"That's life though, isn't it? It never really turns out the way you planned," Cassie said.

Her response sounded like defeat.

Frankie knocked on the table with his knuckles. A family trait. "I'm just asking if Jake is happy. He still blushes around you, Cassandra. There's stuff to talk about if that's still how he feels."

Cassie eyed Frankie and bit her lower lip.

"I know," she whispered.

Jake stared toward the table as he gripped the edge of it. Did Frankie know about the kiss or was his draw to Cassie just that palpable to everybody? Maybe Frankie was using the past evidence to tease him. Even though his brother wasn't in Lovestruck for long that summer, Frankie had witnessed Jake's first meeting with Cassie at a Smith family dinner. He'd even commented that Cupid had hit Jake on the bullseye with the way he'd acted toward her—tongue-tied but stubborn to admit it. Frankie had asked Cassie out on a date *for* Jake when he hadn't had the guts to do it. Frankie's support should've looked like a brother helping a brother. Instead, it had been patronizing. Not that Jake wasn't grateful; he did get the date and the girl. He wished he could blame Frankie for losing the girl, too.

But that was all Jake.

"Enough of this. What's everyone doing?" Cassie scanned the table, hand on her hip. She smiled at his mom, who winked in response, muttering how 'everything's going to be all right.'"

"Walking down memory lane," Frankie answered

Cassie's question. He glanced at Jake again before flicking his gaze back to her. "Have a seat. We're getting to the pictures with you in them."

He pulled out a chair.

Jake's hands dropped from the table and fisted in his lap. He took another grape to keep quiet. They tasted as ripe as Cassie's lips had, which shot his "calm down" plan to hell. Kissing Cassie had awakened a beast that wouldn't shut up now.

"Thanks, but I'm under specific orders to get outside and play." Even so, Cassie walked around the table and sat. "I suppose I can stay for a couple minutes."

His mom handed him another picture, but he didn't look at it. Instead, he slumped against his seat. It'd seemed like days since this morning. Weeks. Years. Cassie had changed her outfit. Now she wore frayed jean shorts and a sleeveless yellow shirt that had little tassel things hanging off the end of the strings. As she stretched her arms over her head, the fabric lifted enough so he could see a hint of her sun-kissed skin.

The quarter moon tattoo near her navel reminded him of the days he'd been blessed enough to see her naked whenever he wanted. Seeing the ink felt like sneaking a peek at something forbidden. If she was his Eve, he'd gladly bite her fruit and be damned to hell.

He was already in hell.

"When would you like me to pick up your pants?" Cassie asked.

Frankie chuckled.

Jake realized she was talking to him after several seconds.

"They're in my tent," he answered. *The scene of*

the crime.

Cassie smirked. Maybe—maybe she was thinking of their kiss, too.

"I'll grab them for you after we're done with these photos," he added.

"Taking your pants off for Cassie again, Jake?" Frankie asked. "You should probably catch up on life first."

Frankie said it so goddamn calmly, it didn't sound like the reprimand it was. He needed to mind his own damn business.

"Don't talk like that," Cassie scolded.

"At least she wanted me pant-less at one time," Jake answered. His mom would stop the argument soon enough. Plus, it was the truth. "You're just—"

"Jacob Hunter Smith." Cassie glared.

He liked when she scolded him; however, he wouldn't give her the satisfaction of admitting it.

Frankie shrugged. "I wouldn't go talking about things you know nothing—"

Cassie elbowed him in the ribcage. "Franklin. Enough."

"Ah." Frankie rubbed the area.

She'd hit him hard, and Jake was proud of her.

"Oh my," his mom interrupted.

Jake grabbed the picture from her hands. It was a family photo—one of the last before his dad died. Everyone held sparklers in their hands, including Cassie, who'd already been with the Smiths for a couple months when the photo was taken. She was kissing Jake's cheek, and he was laughing so hard his eyes were closed. He had his hand wrapped around her waist in complete ownership of who they were to each other.

Jake rubbed his chest with his free hand. His heart had been so sure of what he'd wanted that he didn't question it back then, just like he hadn't questioned his ranching dream. Life had been too easy. He should've realized tragedy was coming. He'd seen enough Western movies to know that. Tragedy often came in one scene. Bing. Bang. Boom.

Frankie wasn't in the picture, and that was normal back then, too. He'd only visited once as Cassie was coming to town, and he'd left swiftly for the next business venture he was attempting to start-up. After that, he came back for their dad's funeral.

He put the picture in the "keep" pile. Everyone was quiet as they continued looking at photographs. There was so much life between his family. Seven years was a long time. He didn't know these people anymore, and they really didn't know him. Each of his interactions the past day were based on who his family and Cassie had been ages ago. But everyone had changed. He had to hit the reset button to survive the rest of this trip.

Frankie stood and left for the bathroom.

Jake relaxed. He was free for a couple minutes because he wouldn't have to worry about what comeback he'd have to be ready to dole out.

"Mommy." Sunny burst into the room, latching to Cassie's neck in one flashing motion. "Come play."

The little girl broke his heart. She was cute as a damn button, and Cassie was sexy as hell as a mom. But this image of them together—he wasn't a part of it.

Cassie patted her daughter's arm before standing and lifting her kid up with her. She grunted as she said, "Any joiners? You know Missy is going to make you all come out eventually."

"No." Jake was injured enough from his stunt work to add any athletic feats to his weekend. The cow fiasco had been enough.

Sunny clasped her hands together and pouted. "Pleeeeease, Jake."

Why on Earth was he wrapped around her little finger? Maybe because she looked just like Cassie with her dimples and her mischievous smile. Boys wouldn't stand a chance when she was older. He braced his hands on the table to lift himself. "What are we playing?"

"Gunnysack races." Sunny clapped.

He closed his eyes and sighed. Men his size didn't hop around like rabbits. They mated like them. Still, he'd do it for the little girl and for Missy. He could act normal. He would act normal.

"Gunnysack races, it is," he mumbled.

This was about to get interesting.

Chapter Eight

Cassie

Missy gave the race directions from the sidelines. Bridget stood next to her, clapping and laughing. It almost brought tears to Cassie's eyes, and it definitely brought a smile to her face. Jake had helped create her smile. Seeing Bridget happy that almost all her loved ones were home was rare. Since Matthew Smith had passed away, it would never again be perfect. Still, this weekend was as close as it was going to get. For once since Jake came home, she didn't want to strangle him with her lassoing skills.

In the kitchen, Jake had shown vulnerability about his life away from Lovestruck. Not much, but enough. Maybe he hadn't left for greener pastures nor was he living a better existence in California, as she'd imagined. Maybe he was enjoying a different life. Jake was the same guy in all the important ways. His cow wrangling earlier proved underneath the pricier clothes and chip on his shoulder, he was in there somewhere. He was a cowboy.

And then their kiss.

She could still taste it on her lips, even though she needed to forget it so she could breathe easier.

She and several other of Missy's and Parker's family members were currently behind a white-painted line on the grass, waist-deep in gunnysacks. The material itched against her calves and thighs. She regretted she'd changed into shorts. She stood between Frankie and Jake, with Sunny standing in front of her as the rest of the kids prepared for heat one. After spending the past couple hours getting the barn back in working order for tonight's dinner and searching through pictures, Cassie was ready to hop.

Or drop.

It had been good between she and Jake in the kitchen. They'd been getting somewhere—her admitting she didn't want him to be alone, and Jake admitting how alone he was. She savored their breakthrough, while keeping her promise to Missy. She was thankful about the promise now. She was a noble friend protecting the truth for the sake of the greater good.

Would anyone buy that excuse?

Frankie had gently attempted the conversation about Sunny while they'd scoured photo albums, even after they'd decided one month ago—Bridget, Kate, Frankie, and her—that ultimately, Cassie would direct the confession. She'd always been in charge when it came to "the situation," and Missy's wishes for her wedding weekend were now in charge, too. So, Cassie shut him down.

She should've resented Frankie for promising to be present for Sunny those first several years when he'd failed to follow through, but she didn't. It was easier on her own.

That is, until Sunny started going to pre-school and asking about her daddy. Plus, Bridget deserved peace within her family, and Cassie didn't want to cause any more pain.

Sunny was warming to Frankie; although, she'd only called him dad once in the past year. She was a girl's girl when it came to relationships. Sunny, Bridget, and Cassie were the three musketeers. Her curiosity about who her dad was remained in theory only.

"On your mark, get set, go." Missy used a blow horn from Frankie's glory days as a football captain to start the kids' race. Cassie clapped as Sunny attempted to hop and progress toward the finish line simultaneously.

"Mommy." Sunny nearly kicked her gunnysack off, throwing a tantrum rivaling Jake's full-on meltdown at the check-in desk yesterday. She stomped her feet and whimpered.

"Forward, sweetie." Cassie demonstrated the art of hop-running for her daughter.

Sunny caught on quickly and scooted forward, nowhere near most of the rest of the pack. But she was at least going to finish.

Cassie felt Jake's gaze on her, and while it was bright outside, the sun wasn't the reason she was sweating.

"What?" She tucked a strand of her hair behind her ear.

He shook his head. "You're good with her. I don't think I could handle parenting."

"Really?"

His words would've resembled a compliment had he not sounded so deflated about it.

She exhaled and crossed her arms.

"It's about wrangling them and feeding them. I

throw in cuddles and bedtime stories." She winked. "You'd do fine."

He dug the toe of his shoe into the grass as he looked down. "You're trying to make me feel better."

"No, I'm saying there's a learning curve for every parent. You should've seen me in the beginning." She opened her mouth to continue but stopped.

"Brandon wins," Missy announced.

The ring bearer, Parker's nephew, celebrated on the far side of the yard. Sunny clapped along with a couple of the other children.

Cassie smiled. She was raising a daughter who bowed healthily to defeat.

"Now for the adult round," Missy exclaimed. She recited the rules again. Basically, no one could purposefully cut off others. Other than that, whoever crossed the line first won. A toe; a nose—anything counted. Cassie's adrenaline pumped so hard her ears sounded like they had the ocean in them.

"Let's go, adult heat!"

She recognized Lester Bott's booming voice somewhere to her right. The guy had been a family friend for years. He was Holy Cross Presbyterian Church's pianist each Sunday, except in the autumn when national football started. Then he was more spiritual and less religious.

"I'm coming for you, Jakey-boy," Frankie said over her head. His tone was playful.

"I'd be careful what you start, city slicker," Jake retorted.

"On your mark, get set, go." Missy announced.

"Shit," Frankie shouted, gathering his sack from his ankles.

"You owe Sunny a dollar," Jake yelled. He was one hop ahead of Cassie, but he gained a second hop as she laughed.

He made the mistake of looking over his shoulder. Thank the universe because she didn't want to play fair. She made her famous "bunny face" at him—her front lip over the bottom one, and her nose scrunched.

He stumbled, his knees hitting the ground before he rolled.

She moved around him easily, underestimating his quick recovery time—no pun intended. Jake was on her heels again in three seconds. His breath and hops were steady behind her while her lungs burned as she pushed forward. She didn't have time for formal exercise these days. She noted to add running every once in a while to her routine.

Sunny's sweet cheers propelled Cassie toward the white line, which would establish her victory. She needed this win in her life.

She tripped, feeling the weight of someone else on her heels.

"Shit." Jake tumbled.

Cassie twisted awkwardly beneath him, struggling to move onto her back. He was now sprawled over her torso. Their chests beat against each other—drums playing a familiar but dangerous song.

She stared, taking in the way his warmth made her shiver all the way to her toes, which were numb from his body on hers. She wanted to grip his hair; to guide his head lower to where she ached to have him touch her; kiss her; cherish her.

A blush spread across her cheeks, but she wouldn't admit his body against hers was as right as believing in the goodness of life. Being frustrated with him was also right. They could've been together, but they weren't.

It wasn't all his fault. It was so easy to blame him, but she was to blame, too.

Jake gazed at her; his eyes wide. "Cass, I—"

He flexed against her hip and grumbled something under his breath, trying to move away from her to hide what she already felt. He could be angry at her; he could be annoyed or frustrated or whatever he thought he had the right to feel this weekend.

He was also turned on.

He detangled himself and stood quickly, bracing his knees.

"Cassie wins." Missy's voice boomed.

"I object." Frankie laughed as he kissed his wife. Kate, who had sat out of the adult round, hugged him around the waist.

Applause erupted, and Cassie stood to curtsy.

"Jake, what just happened?" she asked quietly. He stepped toward her warily as the adults and children scattered to prepare for the groom's dinner.

She flicked her gaze toward his groin. "I *felt* you."

It was the second time today. He'd also had a tent when they'd kissed earlier. Third time would not be the charm.

Jake stared, refusing to hide the way his breaths were strong enough to make his chest rise and fall rapidly. Still, his fists were clutched at his sides. In his navy button-up shirt and blue jeans he'd changed into, the man looked every bit of who he was.

A cowboy. A reluctant cowboy.

"A confession, Cass." He ran his hand through his locks, setting off a thousand fantasies of her doing the very same thing.

"Jake."

Her chest was an empty cavity as she exhaled wholly. She could pretend she didn't have things to confess, too. She could ignore she felt things which would require a panty change later. She could explain she'd met someone at Lushes Pub on her way to Missy's house the summer that changed everything. She could hope Jake's time away would soften his response to the truth.

But he'd more likely hate her.

And he'd probably kill Frankie.

The fact was that maybe even after the wedding, the timing wouldn't be right for them to be okay with each other. Sometimes timing was never right. That was why Romeo and Juliet never ended up together. Timing. Ill-luck. Tragic flaws. A whole lot of drama.

"How badly did I break your heart when I left?"

Cassie could hear Sunny's giggles approaching.

"That's dirty laundry," she whispered. "So is your erection."

Which was now gone.

Sunny hugged Cassie around the waist.

She patted her daughter's arm and stared at Jake. He seemed lost in thought—serious and broody. His hair moved lightly in the wind. He wasn't trying to look attractive, and that was utterly annoying. Because...wow. He was the most handsome man she'd ever encountered, a mix of broodiness and gentleness. The perfect blend of life.

Her chest ached.

"How badly?" he repeated.

"All this time, I thought I could quantify heartbreak

by how many days I've survived it. It's more complicated than that, Jake."

"So you don't know."

"No." Cassie lifted Sunny.

"You don't know what, Mommy?" Sunny asked.

"I don't know how I fell during the race. Isn't that silly?" She gave Sunny an Eskimo kiss and turned away from her ex.

Sunny smiled. "Jake tripped you."

She laughed lightly at the different degrees of truth in her daughter's response. Cassie glanced over her shoulder at Jake as she ambled away. "You're so right, Sweetie. You are too right."

Chapter Nine

Jake

This resetting-the-tone-thing with Lovestruck was as hard as riding a bull—which Jake had done successfully in his life. He'd asked Cassie a serious question—this after he'd owned his erection like a man.

How badly did I break your heart when I left?

Cassie, despite wanting to talk earlier, seemed to have her own reset. She didn't want to talk about anything anymore. He couldn't entirely blame her. His question was bold and arrogant. Public. He hadn't meant it to be.

He bee-lined it to his tent after the gunnysack races.

"Pain in the ass," he mumbled, chuckling afterward at the sound of his soft droll, which had come back with his frustration.

Women changed like the wind. He grew up around his sister long enough to remember. He gathered his shampoo and wash combo and towel, sulking as he meandered toward the fancy, communal pop-up bathrooms for guests. He was used to this type of accommodation on movie sets throughout the years.

Inside the space, the bathroom smelled like clean air and minty bodywash. The toilets were in a separate area. A couple of the shower stalls were being used but a half-a-dozen were empty. He went to a stall near the front, pulled back the white, linen modesty cloth, and turned the faucet forcefully to hot. Being under scorching water felt right. He scrubbed shampoo into his hair and let the suds fall over his face—eyes closed. Images flashed on the backside of his eyelids. All of them—Cassie.

The door opened and shut, but he didn't hear footsteps over the water. He figured it was one of the men across from him leaving.

"Frankie?"

Had he imagined Cassie's voice?

"I'm just finishing. Did Kate send you to look for me?" Frankie said.

"She did. She's setting out the cupcakes and wants you to hurry your behind up."

"So, she wants to avoid my impossibly charming advances." He chuckled.

"You're such a guy."

Jake smiled at her words. He turned off the shower and toweled off quietly. Cassie sounded like a sibling talking to Frankie, keeping him in line. Much of his mom had rubbed off on her.

Still, Cassie was beautiful and while Frankie was married, he had eyes. That was a terrible thing to think about Frankie, who, despite being annoying as hell, was always loyal to his girlfriends growing up.

"You mean a smart guy who loves his wife," Frankie answered.

Jake peeked over the white curtain. Cassie stood in the back of the bathroom, hands on her hips. She was still wearing her jean shorts and yellow sleeveless top. Her hair was down now. He wanted to grip it as he pulled her into the stall for a kiss; a hug; whatever she would allow him. He'd allow her to do anything in return.

"Your equally smart wife needs to get ready, Frankie, and you need to pick up the mints and corsages for your mom and Parker's mom. They should each have a single pink rose and baby's breath. Are you listening?"

The shower curtain flew open. Frankie emerged with a white undershirt on and a towel around his waist. Jake ducked.

"Do you really think mints will be missed?" he asked.

"I don't have time to argue with you about the importance of good breath. I still have to finish Jake's pants to mend for tomorrow along with fifty million other things."

"Have you guys talked seriously, Cassie?"

There was a long pause.

"The kitchen table discussion was about as deep as it's gotten," she finally admitted. She was hard to hear over the running water of the other shower.

"Cassie, you know you need to tell him."

"I'm going to. Missy wants the wedding to happen first. She's only learned about everything herself."

"That's not the only reason you're avoiding, and you know it." Frankie's voice was firm. "I can see it in the way you still look at him. Like you're trying to protect him."

"Frankie, it's not that, it's—"

"Cassie, this effects the entire family. And I've been taking your lead on the matter since it's a sensitive topic, but it has to happen. Now."

"I know." Cassie paused. "It's just so life-changing.

Jake was tempted to peek over the shower curtain again, but he didn't have the balls—or the restraint of his balls—to.

Life-changing. What could be so life-changing? What was Cassie trying to protect him from that the rest of the family would be a part of as well?

His heart beat faster. The only thing he could think of was the land. Maybe Cassie was thinking about selling the Smith property, which would affect the entire family. She'd said at I Do Boutique that she was busy. He understood firsthand how much work a ranch was to run—dude ranch or not. It had scared him out of town. Her secret—and the thing she was waiting to talk to him about—had to be about the Smith land. She was finally ready to sell it, and she wanted him to know. She wanted everyone's blessing. That had to be it. She was asking for freedom.

He listened to Frankie's and Cassie's footsteps as they left, and the place became mostly silent except for one lone ranger still showering.

What Cassie had said to him in the kitchen was true for her, too. She deserved a life. A dude ranch wasn't her passion. Cassie loved creating things. She wanted to design. She was damn attractive in the boutique earlier around all those pretty things. Her dreams weren't passing ones. Jake had listened to her talk about them when they'd been younger. He'd quietly been terrified that those dreams would take her far away from him.

Funny how life worked out.

He couldn't imagine the Smith land not belonging

to someone who loved the family or was part of it. But he would have time to let the truth settle into his bones because, as Cassie had told Frankie, she wouldn't approach him until after Missy's wedding.

He walked to his tent and dressed for the evening. The shower water, scalding and harsh, was supposed to relax him, but like every other second in this town, it had done the opposite. If his family's land was going to be sold, at least it would likely be turned back into mostly ranching land, probably by a neighbor who wanted to expand. Land meant something in Nebraska. It was currency.

Jake hadn't worried about the Smith ranch's fate when he left it behind. Now, though, his gut gnawed at him as he combed his hair. He had to swallow hard to keep his emotions from escaping him. He sniffed harshly.

The fact was he'd been gone a long time from this place, and Cassie had done a fine job holding onto it long enough for him to say good-bye.

What a gift she'd given him.

A proper good-bye.

He would give her his blessing to let go.

Chapter Ten

Cassie

Tailoring Jake's pants while thinking of the beautiful man who'd be wearing them was a hard feat. Still, this was her happy place—with fabric between her fingers. Missy's wedding planning had offered her more opportunities at I Do Boutique and at home working with dresses and jewelry.

Her hair was in curlers for the groom's dinner, and her dress hung above her bedroom door. She wore a bathrobe and slippers as she worked, not the silky kind that cinched at the waist in an elegant way. Her bathrobe was the puffy kind she had to pull harshly to appear like she had a womanly form. Mostly, she resembled a marshmallow.

After her conversation with Frankie, she rushed home to shower. Bridget had Sunny, which gave Cassie a couple extra minutes to herself.

What a mistake.

She sat in her guilt without any distractions. She had been lost when she'd first arrived in Lovestruck as a young and stupid girl. Still, she was proud of Sunny. She'd never wished for a different outcome because her daughter was worth every moment of complication.

But how should she handle Jake? What was right?

She hadn't hidden in a long time.

She finished his pants and was halfway done taking out her curlers when the doorbell ding-donged, interrupting a particularly powerful part of a country song she was listening to.

She rushed too quickly to open the door.

"Hey, Jake." She grabbed the top folds of her robe. Her quest to look casual suddenly felt like she'd given up on life. He stared from her bare ankles up the fabric of her robe to her head. She grimaced at the sight he was taking in. Maybe she should slam the door in his face and start over.

His hands were deep in his pockets, and he rocked on his heels, holding back a smile. His hair was slightly damp, and his clothes fit him as if they'd been tailored for his body—a pair of navy slacks and a maroon, white, and navy plaid button-up.

"You look—" He stopped.

"Exhausted?"

He shook his head.

"Old."

He chuckled. "You look pretty."

She rolled her eyes as she opened the door wider for him. "Don't be mean."

He turned and walked backward, stopping at the wooden staircase in the foyer and leaning against the sturdy railing. "I'm being honest, Cassie."

"Oh." She bit her lip. "Thanks, Jake."

"You're welcome." He chuckled. "I especially like the hair curlers."

She rolled her eyes, smirking. "You're teasing me."

His expression turned serious. "No. You've always been pretty just natural like this."

She bit her bottom lip.

When she'd first arrived in Lovestruck, she couldn't fathom being barefaced, an insecurity from being raised by a beauty-pageant-queen-turned-politician mother. Now, she only wore makeup on special occasions. Like having Jake in her home after seven years. In a way, his presence felt as reverent as Christmas. She wished she had blush on so she could blame it for the color spreading across her cheeks. She also wished she had panties on underneath her robe.

She tugged at the fabric to hide her modesty. Luckily and unfortunately, Jake had already moved on from checking her out.

"My mom reminded me you lived here now." He glanced around the space, which hadn't changed much since he'd left. Cassie had modernized the kitchen and redid the bathrooms when she'd converted the house from the ranch hand's quarters to her permanent address. She was the main ranch hand now, along with Bridget, several local high schoolers, and a couple of townies who didn't want to see the old Smith place fall into Mr. Gregg's hands. The surrounding area had become a tourist destination the last four years after a movie starring one of the biggest "it" actresses had been made on Mr. Gregg's nearby property. He touted his famous home on a billboard along the highway running north. Most people only wanted to make one stop when they passed through Lovestruck. Mr. Gregg's ranch usually won.

Maybe she should invest in children's rides to compete. Still, Matthew Smith had wanted his land to be a ranch. Cassie did her best at her own version of his wish. She hadn't learned a lot of positive lessons from her mother, but one thing she'd always said was, "whatever you are, be a good one." It was an Abe Lincoln quote.

She passed Jake as she walked to the kitchen for caffeine. He followed her.

"It's amazing what you've done to this room." He stopped at a pile of mail on the rustic wooden table next to a floor-to-ceiling window. The cabinets were painted ivory and all the appliances had been replaced. She'd also added hanging lights over the marble countertop.

Despite the house updates, he focused on one letter from the bank. Underneath the letter was a stack of older mail. A cold sweat broke across her cheeks and forehead.

Cassie reached for two mugs, pretending to struggle so he would help her and forget about the mail. Luckily, it worked. Yet again, his cowboy nature showed through. He was as chivalrous as ever even if he resented the panty-dropping quality.

How many women had he shown this kindness to in seven years?

Jake approached her and without reaching on his tippy toes, as she did every day, he grabbed the drinkware easily. It was such simple acts that made her miss him, and she didn't want to miss him. Not when he'd be leaving for California again, hating her more than when he'd arrived.

Maybe all she truly missed was a man. Any man.

It was easy to forget Jake had a life somewhere else when he was in her kitchen; a life she knew nothing about, except for the small tidbits Bridget was able to gather over the years and the few comments Jake had made since his arrival. He could have a dog he kenneled for the weekend; he could have a mansion; he could have a woman who refused to join him for a wedding in a small town. He'd said he was single, but it didn't mean he wasn't mingling. He was thorough in the way he'd kissed her earlier today. Well-practiced. Jake clearly wasn't a man removed from the art of seduction.

She turned too fast.

"Ah." She grabbed the back of her neck. Tingling warmth spread across her shoulders.

"Here." Jake moved her hair away and massaged her neck. It was an intimate gesture, but holy moly, he was gifted. She'd already shown self-control once in ending their kiss in the tent. That could be her one good choice of the day. She'd allow herself a pass to enjoy.

"You're too awesome at this."

"I got bad whiplash on a car stunt I did during The Matchmaker. The set's PT showed me how to rub it out effectively."

Cassie barely heard him. She groaned as his thumb brushed against her skin, easing her tension in one way and awakening tension in another. Her thighs brushed together, and she closed her eyes as she clutched the edge of the cool counter. Her robe was probably open at this point, but she didn't care anymore.

"Jake."

He didn't stop until her shoulders relaxed and the tingling sensation of whiplash subsided. When his hands dropped to his sides, she exhaled and opened her eyes, blinking several times. He moved to the other side of the counter without a word. His footsteps were heavy, as if the moment had affected him, too. Actions weren't enough anymore; she needed the conversation she couldn't have until after Missy's wedding.

"Thanks for that," she said in soft tone, pouring the fresh brewed coffee into her "Best Mom Ever" mug before beginning to pour a second cup.

"I don't drink coffee."

She frowned because she *knew* that. He was a beer-after-work kind of guy; a soda and water drinker throughout the day. Judging from his body now, he'd cut the soda out and taken to light beer. The man didn't have an ounce of fat on him.

Bastard.

Suddenly, she was self-conscious about the soft rolls she had across her stomach, not that he would ever see them. But she saw them. Every night. Her mother would be appalled at the woman Cassie had become if she ever thought to visit the town in the "middle of nowhere." Instead, she'd sent money quarterly but had stopped two years ago, when Cassie sent the money back. No attachment to her mother was best. That was a sad truth to learn. Not all moms were the same.

She shook her head. "I should've remembered."

"What do you remember?" He sat on the same tin stool Sunny did when she ate her breakfast. "About us."

Cassie gazed out the double windows over her sink. Outside various shades of green made up the foreground and the middle ground of the picturesque late afternoon. The sun dipped below the land, casting shadows on the pretty picture but not on her memories. She glanced back at the counter, honing in on a leftover crumb from Sunny's breakfast. Cassie had been rushing, trying to get to the boutique. She hadn't had time to clean up.

"You start," she whispered.

"Riding horses for hours on Sundays," he answered readily. "I still do that if I can get out of the city."

"You do?"

He nodded.

"Alone?"

"Mostly," he answered.

The truth—mostly—hurt because it didn't mean never.

"My friend, Chuck, comes with me sometimes."

"It's none of my business."

"But it's the truth."

The truth. *Tell him. Tell him the truth.*

"Going into town for ice cream." She moved on with a very different truth than the one pounding in her chest. "I loved sharing ice cream with you."

"You hardly shared." Jake chuckled. "I had to fight for every spoonful."

She flicked the crumb at him.

"I remember never wanting to let you go," she said.

"I remember always wanting to protect you." He smiled. "And, of course, the Fourth of July festival."

She still attended the festival with Sunny—where cotton candy and popcorn were staples, along with a parade, yard games, turtle races, and an old car show. Missy had dreamed about emulating the festival for her wedding weekend.

"The Fourth of July festival," she repeated. She couldn't touch the other thing he'd said about protecting her. He'd always been the best at it, shielding her with his blinding, innocent, stupid love.

"This all could've been our life, Cass." Jake hit his knuckles against the counter. "I sure fucked it up."

"No." She licked her lips, appreciating the way

they tasted like coffee now. It was something she could focus on instead of the bitter flavor of regret. They both had fucked it up. He didn't know half of the story.

"Or maybe we would've killed each other by now," he added.

"Probably." She held her mug tightly. Her smirk faded as he came around the counter again. His heavy steps matched the pounding in her ears. He took the cup from her hands and set it down on the marble top. Then, his fingers were on her cheeks, cupping her face. His palms were either cold, or she was hot. Her skin tingled.

"Dammit," he muttered.

"What are you doing, Jake?"

"I want to tell you it's okay to let go."

"Of what exactly?" There was a long list.

"All this." He glanced around the room before returning his gaze to her. "I heard you talking to Frankie about needing to tell me something, and you mentioned earlier to me how hard it is to do all you do. That has to be what you two were discussing. The land. This place. This life. It's not why you came to Lovestruck."

Jake let her go and ran his palms through his hair. It was frustratingly sexy. "Look, I appreciate you caring about it and tending to it. I sure do."

"You don't think I can handle it?" she asked.

"I don't think you should have to if you don't want to anymore."

He stared intensely as if trying to read her.

"Jake, I have a daughter." She got the already obvious out in the open as she collected herself. She couldn't think straight. How could she begin this conversation? Here, in her home, the truth was safe. She couldn't mislead him when he thought her secret was about land. Timing didn't matter. Missy would forgive her.

"And Sunny's not mine."

She shook her head. "No."

"You moved on quickly, Cassie."

No. No. Not true.

"Jake, it's complicated. I—" She almost stepped closer and wrapped her arms around his waist to absorb all the ways he'd become more of a man since he left. That sounded like a lovely idea.

But she couldn't.

Whatever had made him leave, she forgave him for because she had a confession that would've made him run. All her efforts to preserve his life had failed. He didn't dream about this place anymore. He didn't want this ranch or her. He didn't really seem to want the truth, either.

He'd chosen to make up his own version that all her secrets were about land. Soil and grass was the only thing connecting them anymore.

Cassie tapped the counter, which didn't provide enough noise to ease the tension in the room. Outside and up the path, dinner was waiting.

"Your pants are folded over the couch in the living room. I need to get dressed."

"Cassie."

She didn't stop until she reached the top of the staircase. "What?"

"Don't you want closure?" His question came out as an exasperated plea.

No, I want a redo; a start over; a second chance.

She pushed those thoughts away.

Jake didn't want those things. He'd said it. He wanted closure.

"Sure," she whispered. "Good-bye, Jake."

Chapter Eleven

Jake

"I didn't mean closure on everything," Jake clarified.

He meant closure on their past. His present lust for her? That was an entirely different, more complicated story. He lingered for several seconds in misery. He didn't blink—not wanting to miss something in Cassie's body language that would give him consent to run up the steps and sweep her into his arms. Two adults needing more.

"I can imagine how hard it's been," he said as an olive branch. "This ranch is a lot for anyone. No one could possibly blame you for selling it."

Cassie didn't move from her spot on the top of the steps. This was a hard good-bye for both of them. He understood that much. The ranch was like a family member. She shouldn't be chained to it, and he had a life elsewhere. He'd built a different dream on purpose. He was trying to be a decent man by telling her it was okay to move forward. He left it behind. She could, too. Closure.

"Okay, then." He dipped his head. "I'll be going now."

Those words were apparently her kryptonite.

He stopped at the door when he heard her quick

footsteps and turned as she tugged on his elbow. Her chest pushed against his, and she pinned him against the wood. Her palms rested against his torso and her fingernails dug gently into the fabric of his shirt.

"Cassie."

She trembled—trembled—as she stood on her tiptoes and brushed her lips against his.

"I hate you." Her words were laced with a pain he absorbed through his skin.

His blood rushed to all the places that felt too good to make logical choices. His hands moved to her cheeks, bringing their kiss deeper, showing her what seven years apart was like for him, too.

He lifted her.

She wrapped her legs around his waist. She was bare because of her now open robe. Christ almighty. He was tempted to explore her body quickly, but he also wanted to cherish this moment. As he continued to nip and suck on her lips and then her neck, he turned so her back was against the door.

She giggled at the thump.

He slid his tongue along hers, and she tugged his hair, apparently returning to the gravity of this moment. One kiss could be considered a slip-up. This kiss proved something different entirely. This was pure desire. It was Cassie and him. It was how life should've turned out. Every memory coursed through his veins. Her curves were more pronounced now; her skin was soft and warm. Her lower back arched away from the door, and he gripped her round, firm ass, shuddering at her beauty. He was hers, and for as long as this kiss lasted, was his, too. It was like being inside a snow globe. He didn't want to be turned right-side up where this moment didn't make sense anymore.

"Why are you trembling like you're scared?" he asked.

He set her down on the hardwood floor, panting like he'd never learned how to breathe while kissing a woman.

Cassie kept her arms wrapped around his torso—barely able to connect her hands behind his back. She nestled her face against his chest, choking up.

"Cassandra." He pulled her body snugger against him.

Her next words hit his core.

"You scare me, cowboy."

He rested his chin on her head, even though her curlers weren't comfortable against his stubble. "I was lost."

His throat was as dry as hay. His short explanation defied everything he'd been told he was when he grew up—strong, capable, and unbreakable. He was the first damn person in his family to break after his dad died.

Cassie pulled away and wiped her nose.

"More, Jake. Tell me more." Cassie walked toward the couch.

He rubbed his hand over his face. Cassie needed more than what he could give and not only in this conversation. She deserved a man who knew how to talk. He blamed his dad for this shortcoming. Matthew Smith had loved Bridget, but he questioned how affected his father would've been if she'd died first. He would've worked harder, forgotten to eat, and probably died of starvation from not being reminded to do so. Maybe that was love, though. Someone to remind another person to eat dinner. Someone who cared.

He blew out a breath.

"All the responsibility of this ranch was going to fall on me." He paused, feeling like an idiot since Cassie had done it and succeeded. There was a deeper struggle in his departure than the pressure of responsibility, however. "I couldn't see a way to make myself happy here when my dad died. I wanted to be him for so long, but when the time came, I snapped. I didn't know how to exist in my life without him."

"I loved him, too," Cassie admitted.

His throat tightened. "I'm no good at explaining."

She smiled, wiping her eyes. "But you just did."

He sat down, letting silence suspend their conversation. He patted his knees like they were drumheads. Cassie watched his hands, never meeting his gaze.

What was she thinking?

"I ran away when my family imploded, too. I get it, Jake. I just never saw it in you to stay away."

His mouth opened and then closed it. He had intended on coming back eventually.

He stopped drumming on his thighs. "You were going to go back, too, but you didn't."

"That's true."

She stared at her hands in her lap. There was something else she needed to say. He could feel it with every heavy breath cycle she produced.

"Cassie." Her name came out as a question.

"I really have to get ready."

He watched her ass as she walked upstairs, following her but stopping in the foyer. When the door of her bedroom clicked shut, he slid down the wall, with his head in his hands and his elbows on his bent knees. Her home smelled like apples and honey. Handmade pictures Sunny had drawn were tacked up where professional pictures might have been in a different house. Cassie was clearly proud of her daughter.

He lowered his head and muttered, "Christ Almighty."

He wanted these drawings in his own home someday. Not Sunny's drawings, but his kid's art. Jake stayed in Cassie's house and basked in it. And mourned for everything he lost by being a dumb man.

"You're still here?" Cassie glided down the stairs, looking like a goddess. How many heart-stopping moments could he have this weekend before he passed out? Tonight, she wore a navy dress that wrapped around itself in the front and tied in the back. It was patterned with small, white flowers which seemed to dance with the gentle creases of the fabric. Her hair laid in waves and was partially clipped back. Her lips were full and light pink with gloss. *Kiss me again*, they screamed.

He clenched his fists and then flexed them so hard his fingers cracked.

"Easy there, cowboy," Cassie said. "We're strangers now, remember?"

"That's not entirely true." His thoughts were on both kisses they'd shared this weekend—the first borne out of anger, and the second borne out of need.

Cassie extended her wrist and handed him a bracelet he recognized. "Since you stayed, you might as well make yourself useful."

"You still have this thing?" He'd given her the simple silver bracelet with her initial on it during a day trip they'd taken on his rare day off from ranching.

"My name's still Cassie."

"You sure that's the only reason?"

She bit her lower lip. "Don't push it, Jake Smith."

He wouldn't, but it was going to be damn hard to keep his word. He was getting somewhere, but there was no roadmap, and he wasn't confident where "somewhere" would lead. Where the hell was this all going?

****

After dropping his mended pants off at his tent, Jake arrived with Cassie to the groom's dinner—not arm-in-arm but close enough to earn several stares. Cassie jumped off that proverbial saddle and headed toward Ms. Cristian as soon as she saw her.

For how detailed Missy's packet was, there was no formal rehearsal on the agenda for the evening. Jake had memorized his timing tomorrow. Only Missy, Parker, and Frankie, the officiant, were practicing while the rest of the guests enjoyed dusk and appetizers. And damn, there was a lot to enjoy.

The barn looked like a country Cinderella story. There were the floral centerpieces Jake had helped his mom with, and the space smelled like a meadow. The ceiling had ivory tinsel and berry-colored silk in a grand star design. White lights covered the high beams above him. A rustic, horseshoe chandelier hung in the center of the space. He hadn't noticed the piece when he'd been on his wrangle-a-cow mission.

"Cassie uses this as an education building." His mother gripped his shoulder. "Isn't it lovelier than a dirty, old barn?"

He chuckled. His mom had never been much for

the animal smells of ranch life. It made laundry tough, along with having messy sons. She'd reminded him of that often.

"What does she teach here, Mom?"

"Ranching. Sewing. Arts and Crafts. Whatever the guests prefer to learn."

He nodded slowly. "It looks like she could turn it into an event center for extra profit. This place is pretty as a pearl tonight."

He didn't know why he suggested the event center idea, given he'd just told Cassie to move on from it. However, the Smith property had potential as a rental place, if she did want to keep it running. The profit might even help with the financial trouble she was supposedly in and maybe debt was the main reason she had to sell. He'd seen enough of the bank notice in her kitchen before she distracted him with her sculpted calves as she reached for her mugs.

How did she get her drinkware down from the cupboard daily?

She needed help around the ranch.

"I've tried telling her to do something else with this place." His mom interrupted his thoughts. "But it's too much work, and I'm not as young as I used to be. I can't help the poor girl as much as she needs."

He wrapped his arm around his mom and pulled her to his side, even though she was almost as tall as him. She patted his torso.

"You look as beautiful as ever." He kissed her temple. Her hair was curled and pinned back, and while it was now silvery blonde, she still looked youthful, due in part to her dimples, which he'd inherited. She wore a lavender pant suit and heels.

"I'm going to sit down." She took his face into her hands and stared at him.

"What?" His cheeks were smashed, so he couldn't annunciate.

"You should cut your hair."

His hair was gelled back tonight, specifically so he didn't offend her. Clearly, it hadn't worked.

"I'm serious. You're not Brad Pitt." She dropped her fingers and walked away.

"But I play him in some of my movies."

She shook her head, and he knew, if she was facing him, he'd see her smirking.

He patted his head to make sure his hair was in place. His family and friends filed in and took their seats for dinner. He assumed the tables were left without cloths to show off the craftsmanship of the hand-built pieces. Flowers adorned every other chair and ribbons held them in place.

Was this the same space a cow almost ruined today?

It was a testament to the townspeople that everything was put back in place for Missy. For Parker. For love. For the damn fairy-tale.

"They took forever to do." Cassie walked up behind him. He'd already seen her tonight, but it didn't matter. Even from his peripheral view, her beauty was literally gut-wrenching. He turned toward her and shook his head. She was the prettiest woman he'd ever seen. Her eyes were deeper brown tonight, and something about her makeup made the shape of them wider. Sunny was with her, wearing a sweatshirt over her purple dress. She had a neon green baseball in her hand.

"What took forever? The place cards or the flower arrangements?" He stared at the little girl as he spoke.

She waved shyly. Sunny didn't look a thing like whoever her dad was. She was Cassie's kid, except for her blonde hair, which resembled the color of hay.

"You a baseball fan?" He forgot his previous question.

Sunny nodded. "I like all sports."

Cassie's arm tightened around her daughter. "I tried showing her lipstick and my old purse collection. She doesn't want anything to do with them."

"Sewing, too." Sunny stuck out her tongue.

Cassie sighed. "My poor sweetie is doomed with a mother who doesn't have a sporty bone in her body."

"I used to play ball with my brother." He extended his hand, and Sunny gave her ball to him. He tossed it into the air and caught it. He did it again. Higher and higher. Sunny giggled when he caught the ball for the last time and handed it back to her.

"Did you see that, Mommy?" she exclaimed. "He spun around twice and still caught it."

Cassie's eyes widened in fake surprise at his athleticism. "I did. He's very talented, isn't he?"

"Will you play with me tomorrow?" Sunny swayed as she looked at him.

He glanced between mother and daughter.

Cassie bent down, revealing a line of cleavage that made his mouth water. "Honey, tomorrow is Missy and Parker's wedding, and then Jake is leaving."

Sunny's lower lip stuck out further than the top one. She resembled a pissed-off mini adult. Like a pissed-off Cassie.

"I'll play," he said.

"Yay!" Sunny jumped.

Cassie looked at him and mouthed something he couldn't decode. He was too focused on her cleavage.

He gulped down desire as Frankie and a woman approached.

"What's this little pow-wow about, Cassie?" Frankie asked. She shook her head as she stood. The other woman hugged her and kissed both her cheeks. She wore a sleek black dress that left little to the imagination. She was attractive, but Jake didn't notice much other than that fact. Brown hair. Big breasts. Athletic legs.

She stepped forward to hug him but put her hand out instead. "We haven't formally met, Jacob. I'm Frankie's wife, Kate."

Ah, the legend—Kate.

Jake took her hand briefly but addressed his brother. "You married above yourself. Well done."

"I like him already." Kate cuddled against Frankie's side as she touched her stomach.

"That's the first compliment you've given me in a while, Jakey-boy."

"Look at my green ball." Sunny held up the ball she and Jake had played with. Frankie took it and threw it into the air.

"He does better tricks." Sunny pointed to Jake.

"He was a very good baseball player. Jake was even better than me," Frankie answered.

Jake's mouth parted. Was his brother admitting he wasn't the best at everything? It was a wedding eve miracle. Not the one Jake necessarily prioritized, but he'd take it.

"He's still as stupid as ever though," Frankie

added, nudging Cassie for support.

She clasped her hands in front of her and avoided eye contact with everyone.

"Can I go with Bridg-Bridg?" Sunny asked, and Cassie quickly nodded. Frankie and Kate grabbed their place cards and headed to their seats, too.

"It was lovely to meet you," Kate said over her shoulder.

Jake waved her off but smiled. It wasn't her fault he was a class-act grump.

"You can't promise a child something you can't deliver on." Cassie poked his arm, clearly needing to get that off her chest after four minutes.

"Jesus, woman." He rubbed the spot she'd touched.

"I'm serious, Jake."

"I'll play ball with her," he answered. "Sunday morning. We can go out to the old elementary school fields."

"You will?" She huffed, blowing a curl off her face.

"I will. I promise."

She unfolded her crossed arms and started for their table. "Can I trust you?"

"Yes, Cassie." He walked with her, but she beelined it for the ladies' room, leaving him in her feminine dust.

"You like my mom," Sunny said.

Jake jumped.

"What are you doing back?" He rubbed his chest. He didn't recognize his high-pitched, puberty-stricken voice.

"Bridget." Sunny held up his mother's place card. She used her finger to help read his mom's name aloud, letter-by-letter.

"I actually just like your mom's dress." Jake partially lied.

She pursed her lips just like Cassie. The kiddo was clearly not convinced.

He crossed his arms.

"Mikey makes the same face at me, and Mommy says it's because he likes me." Sunny scurried toward his mom.

The kid was too smart for her own good.

He meandered toward his table, stopping when anyone talked to him. It took fifteen minutes to get to his seat, and he knocked his forehead against the table when he sat down—ridding himself of the same questions about Cassie, about leaving Lovestruck, about coming home. A pat on the back interrupted him.

"Trying to lose brain cells?"

Jake grumbled at Mr. Karl's voice, although he reckoned his old neighbor hadn't heard him.

"Something like that," he answered louder.

"You get your britches all mended?" Mr. Karl sat down in the empty seat next to Jake.

Jake lifted his head and sat back in his chair. "I did."

"Cassie does a good job with her sewing."

"She does." He hoped his short rebuttals would spur Mr. Karl to take a hike to his table.

"Ms. Cristian wants to eventually sell Cassie the place, you know. The boutique on Main Street."

"What a great opportunity," Jake answered. He meant it, too. Cassie was in her element when he'd seen her at I Do Boutique. It would be a natural progression for her to run the place. She likely already did much of the work. She loved dresses and all things fashion-oriented.

"It would take giving up the ranch, though. Pearl and I see her every morning before dawn and the lights don't go off until darn near two a.m. How can she add any more to her plate?"

"She doesn't need to keep the ranch," Jake said, moving uncomfortably on his chair.

Silence stopped the conversation for a couple moments.

"You know, a lot of us suspected Sunny was yours," Mr. Karl mused. He grabbed a napkin from the table and wiped his eye. "She has your hair color."

Jake assumed the "a lot of us" was Lovestruck. He leaned forward and placed his forearms on the table as he stared toward the ground. His sex life was no one's business. Cassie's sex life was not up for debate, either, no matter how he cringed about it.

"I'd never run out on my child," Jake replied with harsher conviction than he'd intended. "My dad didn't raise me to chicken out of responsibility."

Something he didn't always honor.

Luckily, Mr. Karl was getting up. His knuckles braced the table, and he grunted as he lifted from the chair, fumbling down onto the seat. Jake put his hand on Mr. Karl's ass to aid him the second time.

Who would help him stand when Jake was older?

As of now, he was on his own.

"Thank you, sir," Mr. Karl said when he got his footing.

Jake gave him a brisk nod.

"Your dad did fine raising two great sons. Frankie has really stepped up, visiting your family. It's nice seeing him in town. Your mom sure does appreciate it."

Jake opened his mouth to ask about Frankie's more frequent visits. Maybe his mom had in fact been sick, even if she didn't look it. A knot formed in his chest, and he couldn't talk—couldn't ask—couldn't become a rooster in the hen wheel always churning in Lovestruck.

Although, Mr. Karl would be a rooster right along with him.

He glanced toward his mother, talking, coincidentally, to Mr. Karl's wife. His mom was older, and she moved slower, but so did Jake. He'd even had to ice his knee after the gunny sack races today. Still, maybe there had been health scares with his mom throughout the years. She wouldn't have contacted him unless something turned out to be wrong, so Jake could've missed something that scared Frankie enough into coming home.

Or maybe Frankie returned periodically to discuss the Smith property.

Jake's gut ached. At one point, long ago, he would've been included in those meetings. He relaxed when he recalled what he'd overheard in the shower. His brother and Cassie were trying to include him now. All he had to do was wait for them to approach him again.

The Ranch's sale was an easier situation to deal with than if his mom were sick.

Several other guests sat and asked questions about his move to Hollywood. They outwardly accepted the answer he'd needed something different in life. They hugged him as if no time had passed. Lovestruck was too good of a town for him.

Maybe he knew that truth all along.

After he'd gone through the buffet line, he got down to the business of eating. People asked more questions, but he stuffed his mouth with barbecue chicken pizza and grumbled his answers, knowing most guests would be too polite to ask him to repeat himself.

They nodded along with his nonsense.

"Hey." Frankie slapped his back.

He coughed as his brother sat down at the empty seat where his plus one was supposed to be. He'd lied to Missy and said he had someone to bring. At the last minute, he'd changed his mind about trying to bribe his agent to accompany him. Now, he was glad he'd been a man about his homecoming. Cassie and he were sort of getting along. She was wearing the bracelet he'd given her. She hadn't tossed it to the wind when he left. That counted for something.

So did their kisses.

So did her tears before tonight's dinner.

Jake stabbed a bean with his fork and shoved food into his mouth. "Wha-do-you-wan-Fwankie?"

He didn't listen to a word his brother said, but he added "uh-huh's" occasionally, and Frankie was appeased.

His eyes glued on Cassie. The room smelled, tasted, sounded, and felt like her. She played with her pearl earring as she laughed alongside one of Missy's friends. Her plate of food stayed mostly untouched. She avoided eye contact, or at least it sure as hell felt like she did. She made a concerted effort to mingle with everyone but him.

It was only eight o'clock when she yawned and hugged Missy good-bye.

"Excuse me." He wiped his mouth with an ivory

115

paper napkin and threw it toward Frankie.

"Hey, man," Frankie grumbled. "I was trying to catch up. You know, be friends. Be bros."

"Later," Jake lied.

He watched as Cassie found Sunny, who ran over to his mom after she'd given Cassie a hug. She snuck out without saying another hour of good-byes to everyone.

He practically scaled the walls to follow her. He waited most of the short walk to catch her shoulder and turn her toward him.

She jumped, clutching her handbag to her chest, while her other hand swatted the air between them.

"Jesus, Jake." She slugged his gut.

He took his hand off her and crouched in pain. Her punch hurt as much as getting hit in the groin, especially after the way he'd stuffed himself at dinner. "Sorry. I wanted to talk to you."

"About what?" She sounded annoyed.

Before he could speak because he was catching his damn breath, she continued. "Maybe about promising my daughter you'd play catch with her. She's going to remember that, you know?"

He straightened slowly. "Are we still on this?"

"It's one thing to disappoint me, but Sunny's a child," Cassie said. "She gets disappointed enough in life."

"Why do you think I'd disappoint her?"

"Seriously?" She took a step closer to him, so he was in her shadow. "It's the hardest thing acting happy tonight with you here and me here and nothing between us."

"Nothing?" he asked. "I wouldn't say nothing."

She shook her head. "Hiding behind closed doors, having hushed conversations. This is nothing, Jake. I couldn't even look at you tonight."

"I knew you were ignoring me."

She rolled her eyes. "I'm disappointed with how dysfunctional we still are, and I don't want you doing the same to my daughter."

"We aren't that dysfunctional. I see a lot of shit in Los Angeles." And that was what he liked about the place. He fit in.

"A couple kisses don't mean anything, Jake."

"You don't trust me." He said it as a bold truth. "You don't trust that those kisses don't mean something to me, just like my promise to Sunny."

There was a long pause.

He ran his hand over his hair, forgetting about the gel, which made the move impossible. "I wasn't trying to disappoint you. Ever. Didn't you hear a word I said before? I left this town because I couldn't handle life without my dad—not to fuck up my life with you. Our relationship was collateral damage."

"That makes me feel so much better," she muttered.

His nostrils flared, and he growled. "My dad was my hero. You wouldn't understand what the loss was like for me."

Tears pricked her eyes. "I wouldn't understand?"

He stepped back as Cassie put a finger to his chest. Her tone was fire. "First of all, Jake, I cared about you, so I would've been there for you if you would have let me." She paused, looking at her feet. When she stared again, tears streamed down her cheeks. She dropped her finger and exhaled.

His chest tightened.

Cassie looked so vulnerable. Young. Broken.

He wanted to hug her, but he'd likely hurt her more if he did.

She cleared her throat. "My mom was my hero. I craved her attention. I did anything to get it. No, she didn't pass away, but she abandoned me after her affair. When I got pregnant, she offered to pay me not to come back. Don't you dare tell me I don't know what it's like to lose a hero, Jake Smith." She dropped her head. "My hero became a villain. It was devastating."

"I didn't think about it like that," he admitted.

Cassie stepped away from him, moving toward her porch steps. "Because we were too busy knocking boots for you to really listen to what I was going through."

"And I suppose that was all my fault, too."

"Of course it wasn't, you big, old martyr. We were just young. Stupid. We were in love without knowing how to handle real life. People in their early twenties just shouldn't do it."

"Fall in love?" he asked.

"It should be a crime."

He chuckled. "That's ridiculous."

She smirked, despite her tears. "Maybe."

"Cassie, I'm sorry." Jake was an absolute bull-headed prick for bringing any of this up to her, even with his intent to help her understand. In reality, all he was doing was justifying his decision, and she served him with a heaping helping of humility in return. She would've helped him through his shit had he stayed. He'd have a lot to talk about in therapy when he returned to California. At his last session, he'd accepted the past without wanting to change it. What a fucking lie.

"That time's over in my life anyway." Cassie propped her screen door open and wiggled her key into the lock. Clearly, she was trying to accept the past, too.

"You have more to say than that." He challenged. Sassy Cassie was usually up for a debate. She turned, and he stepped up onto the porch—ready for a slap. A hug. Another kiss.

He had followed her tonight with the hope of more *anything*. His hope was extinguished with the wariness in her eyes. She wasn't going to let him in, and he didn't mean into her house. Their kisses were supposed to move them past some of *the* past. For closure on a negative time in both of their lives.

Kiss and make up was an actual damn adage. But did he really want to make up? Or was he just mad she had more control over his heart than he did?

"I do promise to play with Sunny. You can trust me on that, Cassie."

Cassie played with her keys. "Okay."

"I want you to believe me." He brushed his fingertips down her arm and gritted his teeth as her chest rose dramatically. What he really wanted to say was he needed her to believe in him. But that would be too much. Seeing her again this weekend was all too much. "Believe my promises."

He was tortured into watching tears prick her eyes again and fall down her cheeks, bringing with them gray shades of mascara.

"You promised a lot of things. I get now how you must have felt when your dad passed. I do. I needed you to stay though, and you can't fix that." She shook her head, growling. "God, I don't deserve to be upset, but I am. Maybe we should let go of holding each other to all those broken things. Let's call a truce."

"I don't want to."

"You want to keep fighting, Jake?"

"I just don't want to let it go. I thought I had, but I was wrong."

Another epiphany.

"You're leaving," Cassie said. "You don't live here anymore."

He exhaled, digging his hands into his pockets because he had no argument. Cassie must've taken his silence as dismissal because she tucked inside, letting the screen door slam and bounce closed.

"I loved you, Cassie." He banged his fist on the frame.

"No, you didn't," she whispered through the screen. "You didn't even know me."

He pounded his hand against the doorframe before resting his forehead against his fist. His were empty words because she didn't believe him. He'd been a damned coward when they were younger, and he was an asshole now.

He never deserved to be a cowboy.

Chapter Twelve

Cassie

People messed up royally.

Cassie was used to it in her life. Her mother's affair; her family's subsequent demise; her surprise pregnancy before falling in love with Jake; her attempt to control her world to no avail. Her life was a class act example of chaos. But the chaos in her heart after the groom's dinner was a different form of torture. It awakened what she'd feared was underneath all her other feelings.

Regret.

She shouldn't have kissed Jake this weekend. Was he irresistible, or was she just hard up for a good make-out session? It had been years since she'd been kissed, and the last time was with the guy who'd re-painted the barn.

Kissing Jake had made any of their other conversations harder to start now. She laid in bed, staring at her ceiling fan as it worked noisily to cool her room. She also had her row of windows open. Outside, the light breeze through the tall grasses kept her thoughts company.

Earlier tonight, she'd run downstairs and pressed her lips against Jake's mouth because she'd been scared. Heart-pumping, spine-tingling scared he would walk away, and they wouldn't speak about anything important again. It was a senseless move. A trick she'd used in her past life to seduce. Jake *was* going to walk away. Eventually at least. He had a life out west. There was no point in getting PTSD over their unfinished business. She'd been living it for years. She'd only complicated it by allowing old feelings to sidetrack her the past twenty-four hours.

She rubbed her temples and groaned.

Why had she cried in front of him?

His departure would hurt just as badly as his first time leaving. She'd only figured out her reality after she'd kissed him. Something still existed between them in a way that made her sick to her stomach.

Life before this weekend was easier. She missed her normalcy, and yet she was terrified to go back to it on Monday when Jake was gone again. Could she really stay in this routine forever? Maybe it was time to do something different. Maybe this weekend was a restart in another way. Instead of finding hope and forgiveness in the truth, she was meant to find freedom in letting go.

Maybe that was a better gift—freedom.

Kicking her quilted covers off the bed, she stomped downstairs and made a cup of coffee. If she were going to be up all night, she might as well have caffeine.

A soft knock on her front door interrupted her sipping and pacing the first floor.

The microwave blinked one-thirty in the morning.

Jake better not have lingered in the bushes. She wasn't interested. Not really. Still, her heart ached every time she and Jake parted, and she hadn't eased it enough by remembering the reasons she hated him, too.

She needed a couple more hours. Plus, she was wearing her favorite yellow duck pajamas, which was only one step up from her puffy robe.

She shuffled across the wood floor and clicked open the door, prepared to send him on his way.

Bridget held up her hand. "I come in peace."

Her other hand gripped Sunny's fingers.

"Mommy." Sunny giggled.

Cassie relaxed her shoulders. She hugged her daughter with one arm as she gripped her mug. "Hi, sweetie. Are you feeling okay?"

"She missed her bed," Bridget explained.

Cassie smiled as Sunny crawled up the stairs and kept moving toward her bedroom as if she was a puppy. That was her latest thing. Puppies. She always named herself Ruff Ruff.

"I think Sunny's in a possessive phase. She's very aware of what's hers. It must be difficult having her daddy living across the country," Bridget said. "She's asking lots of questions about whether I'd still love her if she ever moved away."

The back of Cassie's neck tingled, and her cheeks warmed. She hadn't done a good job making sure her daughter wasn't around when she'd been on the phone with Missy's friend, conversing about the job opportunity in New York weeks ago.

She turned toward the kitchen. "Having a daddy live so far away is a big deal. This year, she's shown more interest in asking questions about him. It's funny, though, because when he's here, she's shy. She clutches to me more. She doesn't call him daddy often, and neither he nor I push her to. It has to be her journey."

Cassie would go along with that reason alone for

explaining Sunny's behavior. The truth remained, however, that she was considering a job outside of Lovestruck.

Tears pricked her eyes because of...everything.

Frankie and Kate's under-the-wraps-for-now baby was a big change for everyone, too, including Bridget who didn't know yet. And for Sunny, who was going to be a big sister and would find out soon. Maybe she sensed it. Kids were empathic about these things.

Cassie fisted her hands as she remembered the conversation. At first, the baby news was strange, bringing to light how not ideal Cassie's own pregnancy was with Frankie. She was now the third wheel in his and Kate's family. The dynamic was just that—dynamic. Sunny would have a younger sibling. Was Cassie supposed to be proactive in making sure they were close? How did this all work? She needed a magical maid to help clean up the secrets in her life. Spit-spot.

She smiled.

"What's so funny?" Bridget asked.

Cassie shook her head. "Just thinking about my need for a magical maid."

"But you have me." Bridget passed her.

"True." Cassie bit her bottom lip. She didn't add that if she sold the ranch, she'd move from Lovestruck as well—a real fresh start; a place which truly was her own, even if it would be lonelier. This meant no magical maid-aka-Bridget.

Bridget remained quiet as she snuck into the pantry. Cassie indulged in a sleeve of Sunny's shortbread cookies, while the town's matriarch decided on nothing and poured herself a glass of fresh lemonade.

"Why are you up so late, dear?"

Cassie shrugged. "Just a lot going on like always."

"I worry about you as if you were my own child."

She nodded slowly, absorbing the truth in Bridget's words. She'd needed to hear them after her conversation with Jake. She hadn't talked about her own mother in years, and it always served as an emotional topic when she did.

Bridget had done a lovely job of being a mentor. She'd nurtured Cassie into the mother she was to Sunny. She shuddered that her next chapter could include moving. But she could leave, and that was something, too. She was capable of handling life on her own. She'd proven it.

She blurted, "I have a potential job opportunity."

Bridget took a long drink.

Cassie crammed three more cookies into her mouth.

"Something other than taking over I Do?" Bridget asked.

Cassie hadn't thought much about I Do Boutique's change in ownership since it was brought up nearly a year ago. Ms. Cristian was asking for too much money in the buyout, and Cassie couldn't own the boutique while paying down her debts from the ranch—a fact less important if she sold it. But seriously considering I Do would mean leaning on Bridget once again to help with Sunny. Bridget deserved to travel, to sit around, to relax.

She had watched Bridget slow down. She wouldn't force her into an early grave by depending on her more than she already had the past seven years. She'd make enough money to have daycare services for Sunny in New York. Plus, there was Frankie within a half day's drive.

"A friend of Missy's saw the fashion blog I created years ago. She has an opening for a brand developer on a new wedding line she's doing." Cassie paused. "I don't know. My blog was silly. It's still silly. I don't work on it much anymore."

She had once spent hours sketching dress designs, purse designs, and jewelry designs. She'd then blog about her process, from start to finish.

"It isn't silly," Bridget interjected. "You shouldn't have stopped doing it regularly."

"When do I have time now?"

Bridget nodded. "True."

"Anyway," Cassie said, "I sent her pictures of sketches I've created throughout the years. She's looking to eventually hire an additional designer, so this current opportunity would likely lead to more of what I love."

"You sound interested in it."

Cassie hadn't shared the news because she was uncertain about it. She hadn't seriously considered New York until Jake's lack of interest in the Smith property urged her to re-examine changing her life. Sticking around Lovestruck didn't win her brownie points from him. She'd unknowingly looked for some sort of validation in her choices, and it had gotten her nowhere.

Maybe she was the martyr.

She accepted that this weekend was an "open your eyes and move forward" lesson.

It was time to imagine a bigger picture.

"New York is a lot closer to Frankie," Bridget added.

Cassie nodded. "I like the idea of being closer to her dad if the job makes sense for me."

Plus, Cassie had always dreamed of a sibling, and she longed for Sunny to have that experience more full-time.

She sighed.

"It might be the right thing to do and the right time to do it. Sunny's not too far into her schooling. She could make friends easily elsewhere." Cassie paused. "But she does love it here. She loves you."

Bridget tried to smile, but the corners of her mouth wouldn't turn up. "My grandbaby is going to be so far away."

"I haven't decided. I don't know what I'm going to do," Cassie answered. Part of her was excited about taking the leap. Once she allowed her heart to be anything else but scared. The move to New York made sense for a certain version of herself. Was she that woman anymore?

"What's wrong?" Bridget walked to her.

Cassie leaned over the counter and took several deep breaths. "I still have this aching throughout my body. I'm exhausted carrying around my feelings toward Jake."

"Jake? What does he have to do with New York?"

She sniffled. "Nothing really. It's just…he doesn't want this place, and I guess I've been hoping for a different outcome. Or a clearer picture of what to do and how to do it. I hadn't realized I was holding onto this life *for* him in a sense." The thought dawned on her like a new sunrise. "I think I'm stuck."

"Do you still love him?"

The question was fair. Cassie was surprised it hadn't come up more often in their conversations. She frowned. "There's no way for me to answer your question well."

"Because you're confused?"

Cassie swore under her breath. "Because I'm not confused. I've always loved Jake." She sniffled again. "Your son is my weakness."

"Maybe you should tell him. Preferably not during Missy's ceremony, but before he leaves. We all know he's hard to get a hold of nowadays." Bridget stared at her. "Have you ever told him how you feel?"

"I thought I had more time to." Cassie turned away, embarrassed. She was supposed to be talking veils, flowers, and cake this weekend, not broken hearts that didn't deserve any reverence. She'd met Jake at a weird, murky time in her life when her parents were divorcing. Her "I love you" would've meant nothing back then. She hadn't believed in it.

She rubbed her forehead.

"All I'm saying is you might want to at some point." Bridget tightened the bun near the nap of her neck—a sign she was disappointed. "I think he'd be tickled by why you stayed. Honesty might even get you what you want in all this."

"I was thinking of telling Jake on my death bed."

Bridget laughed. "Or mine. It's coming quicker."

"Don't joke about that." Cassie's eyes welled. She was an emotional wreck this weekend, after not crying for years. Maybe she could convince Bridget to move to New York with her. She'd be close to Frankie's family, Parker and Missy, and Cassie and Sunny.

Still, Matthew Smith was buried in Lovestruck. Bridget would never leave him. Plus, the town was her community. Her life. Her world. In many ways, Lovestruck was all Cassie really knew, too. She'd grown-up in this town. She'd not considered leaving it once Sunny was born, but she'd also been dependent on Bridget.

Her stomach ached and not because of the sleeve of cookies she'd eaten. "I have to tell Jake about Frankie first. He might not even care about my 'I love you' after he hears what we did."

"You didn't do it to hurt him, Cassandra."

"I know. Frankie and I never meant to hurt anyone. It was one ill-judged night right before I met Jake."

"Bigger things have happened in my family than your pseudo love triangle."

Cassie rolled her eyes. Bridget acted like it wasn't a big issue; although, she'd had a long time to adjust to the family's reality. She'd taken the news hard at first. However, once a person was living in it long enough, the situation wasn't overly outlandish. It was a horrible coincidence that her one-night stand had been with Jake's brother.

"I slept with Frankie. How do you think he's not going to hate me for that?" Cassie threw her hands in the air. "I slept with two brothers. I'm like—a—tart. A Greek Tragedy."

"Or a comedy," Bridget answered.

She pursed her lips. "That's not funny."

Bridget sighed. "He will hate you for a while."

Cassie nodded. "Exactly."

"But remember, you hated Jake for a while, too," Bridget said. "And you're over that."

"Who says?"

Bridget raised her eyebrows. "You think I don't know you've kissed this weekend. Starstruck is written all over the both of you."

When Cassie wouldn't admit she was right, Bridget set down her glass. "My childhood best friend married her ex-fiancé's brother. You didn't go that far."

Cassie's eyes widened. "Mrs. Brooks almost married Richard the butcher?" She paused, absorbing the information. "Now I feel bad that we all gossip about Richard for making every conversation about meat."

Bridget laughed but stifled the sound with her hand. "Haven't you ever noticed how the family never gets together on any holiday? They make us look normal."

"I just figured no one liked Richard."

"True, but that's not the only reason there's trouble," Bridget clarified. "Richard does deserve a little compassion from us. He got his heart broken."

Cassie buried her face in her palms. "The problem is I don't regret my choice. Frankie and I have a beautiful daughter. That's what Jake will need to get over. I don't regret what happened because of Sunny."

"Guess what?"

"What?" Cassie mumbled.

"It's all going to be okay." Bridget glided toward the front door. "Fake it until you are okay, Cassie. Just like I did when my Matty died. One day, you'll almost feel normal again."

She followed Bridget, her hand on her back. She stopped and hugged the matriarch in the small foyer. "You're right. This must be such a hard weekend for you, too, and here I am making it about me."

Bridget pulled away. "You're a good distraction."

Cassie shut the door quietly behind her.

Bridget had been busily trying to make sure everyone else was okay this weekend, when she, too, was struggling. For the family's sake, Cassie would fake the crap out of her situation. She'd pretend she had everything she wanted. The act should be easy. She'd been performing it for seven years.

But could she ever say "I love you" to Jake? Did she deserve that chance? What did she expect Jake's response to be?

She trudged to the kitchen and ate another sleeve of cookies.

****

Her head throbbed because of the morning's commotion. She should've consumed more caffeine. She also should've given Missy a sedative.

Watching Missy pace her parents' old bedroom, today's bridal suite, was a whole other level of Tums-inducing chaos. The photographer had already captured one meltdown over a failed attempt at makeup contouring. Now, Missy was in the corner, staring out the big window, with a brown bag to her mouth. This was a far cry from the happy, calm Missy yesterday. She choked in and out. This situation couldn't be about Parker. They'd seen each other at breakfast. Did Missy suddenly think it was bad luck to share a banana and eggs with the groom?

"Mommy?" Sunny tugged at Cassie's dress. "Why is Auntie Missy crying?"

Cassie squeezed Sunny's shoulder and led her toward the door. "Let's have you go downstairs, honey."

Sunny continued staring at the train wreck in the room, so she picked her daughter up and set her back down when they'd reached the top of the steps. Sunny folded her arms and pouted.

"People sometimes cry at weddings, sweetheart," she explained. "They're happy tears."

"They don't look happy," Sunny answered, though she did drop her arms to her sides. A child's version of surrender.

"What do happy tears look like?"

Sunny used her pointer finger to tap her chin. Her eyes lit up. "I know. They come with a smile."

Cassie bit her bottom lip. "You're right. Tell you what, why don't you go downstairs and make sure everybody's ready, and we'll be right down? Make sure you find Kate and stay with her."

"Okay." Sunny obeyed this time.

"Don't ruin your dress," Cassie said to Sunny's back. She turned and re-entered the bedroom again, busying herself with steaming Missy's veil. She could handle clothes better than people. New York sounded good at the moment.

Bridget rubbed Missy's back, begging, "Darling, please calm down and tell me what's wrong."

The Smith matriarch was already dressed in her dusty blue pantsuit—a symbol she was both the mother and father figure in the Smith family. Her hair was down and curled, an antique comb holding half of it back. She'd worn the same hairpiece on her wedding day.

When a couple minutes passed, and Bridget was no closer to soothing Missy, Cassie set the steamer down and returned to the meltdown.

"Missy, I know it's a big day. Just keep thinking of who you're marrying. You love Parker. It's going to be wonderful."

She closed her eyes and held back her emotion. Her own almost wedding had been at twenty-one-years-old at the courthouse, signing papers simply because it was the "right" thing to do. Her belly had been big. She'd worn ivory. Frankie, thank God, had finally convinced her it wasn't good to promise forever to each other. He'd made a different vow instead to be there for Sunny as he learned how to be a dad.

Missy shook her head, hugging the hankie Cassie embroidered for her with an *M* and a *P* on it, along with a sunflower.

"What's wrong?" Cassie softly urged.

"Dad's not here." Missy sniffled against the fabric, looking only at her mother even though Cassie had asked the question. "He should be here."

"You're right. Your dad should be here." Cassie bit her lip. Weddings were awful in that way. They highlighted all the reasons to be thankful for love while never letting its guests forget the inevitable truth that love was lost, too. This wasn't a meltdown Missy was having. It was a reality check in the midst of her fairy-tale.

Missy and Bridget embraced as Cassie bent down to straighten Missy's dress. A soft knock on the door interrupted the moment.

Missy's other three bridesmaids were downstairs waiting for the ceremony to begin, leaving Cassie alone on door duty. She scrambled over to the oak double doors and opened them to the vision of so many of her dreams and nightmares.

Light brown cowboy boots.

Dark brown slacks tailored perfectly to show off his calves.

An ivory button-up dress shirt with a crooked burgundy tie.

A suit coat, highlighting his male broadness.

A clean-shaven, tanned face.

An ivory cowboy hat.

Jake had tried most of it on in front of her yesterday morning at the boutique, but she still held her breath as she admired him. Her tongue darted between her lips.

Jake licked his lips in reply, making no apologies as he checked her out. His stare stopped on the modest amount of cleavage the sweetheart neckline of her dress allotted. She'd tailored it well. Mental pat on the back.

He licked his lips again. "You look heartbreakingly beautiful."

"Oh hush," she whispered. No matter how frustrated she was, his compliment still melted most of her defenses. They always had.

She glanced at his chest. "Let me fix your tie."

Chapter Thirteen

Jake

"You can exhale." Cassie flipped the tongue of his tie toward his nose.

He chuckled, and his shoulders relaxed even as his awareness of her sent his blood moving quicker throughout his body. Cassie was in a strapless burgundy dress that matched his tie. Her hair was curlier than last night and tucked in a low ponytail, wisps of it around her face. She had hardly any makeup on, but she glowed in the already bright hallway.

Her eyes were damp.

"Everyone freaking out?" he asked.

With a pat on his chest, Cassie finished his tie and stepped back to examine him. "Missy's upset your dad's not here."

He pushed his hand into his pocket. "Shit."

The air conditioning unit was the only sound in the space between them for several seconds. Jake ran his free palm behind his neck. Missy had dreamed of Dad walking her down the aisle, and he was inadequate. Once again.

He'd come into this day with more hope than he'd had in a long time because he was figuring out his emotions.

Six words changed that. *Missy's upset your dad's*

not here.

"Excuse me." He kissed Cassie's forehead and moved into the room. "Mom, can you and Cassie give us a minute? We'll be right down."

His mom hugged him.

"You look just like your father," she whispered against his cheek. She didn't mention his hair today. When the doors clicked shut, and both she and Cassie were gone, he turned toward Missy.

"You look stunning." He hugged her gently, not wanting to mess up her dress. "When did you go and grow up?"

Missy rested her chin on his chest and whispered, "I miss Dad."

"I miss him, too." He'd never admitted that out loud to anyone in such a blunt way. He had to clear his throat before he could speak again. "And I know I'm not him, but I'm really honored to walk you down the aisle."

Missy stayed quiet as his eyes welled. He coughed gruffly. "Shit. I don't know what else Dad would say to you. All I know is that Parker is a lucky guy."

His sister moved her face, so her cheek rested on his chest. She hugged him tighter. "That's why I wanted you to fill in. You're just like Dad."

"The emotionally-challenged part?"

She laughed through sniffles. "Well, that, but all of the other stuff, too. The hat, the walk, the attitude. You even smell like him."

"I smell like soil?"

"What?"

Jake shook his head. "To me, Dad always smelled like the earth—soil—man."

He discreetly sniffed his armpit.

Missy pulled away. "You only saw Dad as a rancher, but there were other things to him. He smelled like clementine to me. And he was a reader. He got up in the middle of the night to read old western novels."

"He did?"

"Everyone has different memories of Dad. We all miss him."

Warmth spread over his face. He hadn't known his father outside of "the business." They'd talked fields and livestock, but it hadn't occurred to him that Matthew Smith was a much different dad to his baby girl.

Missy was right. Everyone who loved their dad grieved him. Just because his entire life had been more intricately woven with his dad's didn't make his sister's pain any less potent—didn't make his absence at her wedding any less devastating. Everyone experienced the loss. Everyone could've leaned on each other. They still could.

"I never realized," he admitted.

"You're a stubborn man." Missy sighed.

Stubborn, but hopefully getting better.

"Before I forget." He pulled out a small box from his pocket and handed it to her. Missy's lips parted when she opened it.

"Something old." He shrugged at the maroon guitar pick. "It was Dad's from when he played with The Crickets."

Missy was wide-eyed. "They're playing at the reception."

"Dad would've loved that. He would've loved everything about today."

Their final moments in their parents' old bedroom were filled with him wiping makeup from his suit jacket, and Missy taking several big breaths and shaking out her hands.

"Ready?" He held out his arm for her.

She smiled, her eyes still glistening. "For the rest of my life? Heck, yes."

As they descended the staircase, Missy asked, "Why did I see you coming out of Cassie's house before dinner yesterday?"

He grumbled at the hint of tease in her voice. "How did you know about that?"

"I see everything," Missy answered. "It's the journalist in me. We watch and listen."

"You mean you spy and eavesdrop."

Missy glanced smugly at her manicured hands. "You can call it what you want, but I have two eyes, and I saw you walk out of Cassie's house."

She was an accomplished journalist. However, she apparently hadn't seen him sneaking out on the groom's dinner. Or before that, Cassie running out of his tent. Both wins.

"It wasn't scandalous if that's what you're asking. I ripped these pants when I lassoed Mr. Karl's cow, and Cassie offered to mend them for me. So I went over to her place to pick them up."

"You ripped your pants?"

"They're fine." He circled to prove it.

"Why didn't Cassie pursue fashion?" he asked once his clothes had passed Missy's keen eye.

Music played in the yard.

The melody drifted in through the windows.

Missy took her rose bouquet from her personal

attendant, who then worked to smooth the back of her dress and retie her bow after Jake had made an abominable attempt at it. He was too distracted waiting for Missy's answer.

"Cassie doesn't talk about it much, but we all have our guesses. She actually made my dress."

He glanced down. Missy's dress, with its delicate beadwork and silk flower appliques, was truly Cassie's creation. He stared at the gown more reverently than he had when he'd first seen his sister. The dress was tastefully strapless and beaded on top with small floral appliques, which added texture he couldn't describe as a knuckleheaded man. Layered fabric created an abundant bottom. Jake had no true clue about clothes. His favorite things to wear were bootcut jeans and white V-neck shirts that came in a pack of three.

Hardly inspired.

But Missy's dress was a work of art. Just like Cassie.

His sister's gown was whimsical and romantic—a fairy-tale personified, like she'd wanted. Cassie needed to make more masterpieces. Why the hell did he feel guilty?

He rubbed his chest, mulling over the passage of time. How much of it had he wasted? How much time had *Cassie* wasted keeping this ranch when she should've been making pretty things?

It was obviously the perfect moment to be thinking of mortality. Still, it was hard not to, knowing he was filling in for his dad.

"I hope you get married one day." Missy lingered at the back door, which led to the ceremony.

"Some guys are meant to be lone rangers." He

stared outside as they waited for the music to change. Cassie had been the closest he'd gotten to the love of his life, and it hadn't worked. It still wasn't working. Every day, people lived and died alone.

"You're not one of them." Jake vaguely heard his sister say.

His intense gaze found Cassie's back, and his breath left him.

She stood in front of Sunny, who wore a crown of flowers as the flower girl. Together, they walked down the aisle, lined with pots of wildflowers leading to an archway made out of a firecracker color scheme of roses. She glanced over her shoulder, and hot damn, he bit the inside of his cheek. Each time he gazed at her, he noticed something more. Now, it was how beautiful her neck was—exposed because of her low up-do hairstyle. The back of her neck was where he'd kiss her first if she'd allow it. He'd drag his lips to her ear and press his mouth there. Then, he'd tug on her lobe before grazing her jawline. He'd find her lips slightly parted and with a small intake of breath, their mouths would meet—first tenderly and then…not so much.

He gulped so hard his Adam's apple hurt.

Behind Cassie was the Smith land—green and alive and worth saving. Everything in front of him was worth saving.

"Here Comes the Bride" started and the doors to the backyard reopened. People stood. He and Missy walked forward slowly. Loved ones smiled at Missy and then at him, stepping in for a father who should've been present. Their thoughts were clear in their stares.

He choked up, digging his free fingers into his thigh to divert his attention.

An audible "beautiful" came from Uncle Travis.

Missy blew out a shallow breath. "Thank you for being here, Jake."

His fingers dug deeper into his thigh. He hushed his sister, so he could walk her the rest of the way without losing his shit. At aisle's end, he pecked Missy's cheek and guided her hands into Parker's, who kissed the top of each one.

"You're perfect." Parker looked at Missy only.

Jake patted Parker's shoulder.

"Take care of her." The words sounded unnecessary, but Matthew Smith would've said them.

He took his dad's place next to his mom.

"Good job." She rested her fingers on top of his in his lap.

He had a lot of making up to do. He was supposed to replace his dad in the family. Run the ranch. At the moment, he ached for that responsibility. He was an undeserving prodigal son today.

Frankie officiated the ceremony. Leave it to his older brother to somehow weasel his way into being a central part of every picture.

"Doesn't she look beautiful?" his mom asked.

Jake patted her knee. She was talking about Missy, but he couldn't keep his eyes off of Cassie. He ached for her attention. When her gaze wandered to him, he winked.

Cassie bit her lower lip, and her stare quickly returned to the main action. She glanced at him again, smirking in answer to the second wink he gave her. From there, the game was on—who could steal the most stares without anyone noticing. It was a tie until the vows, when Cassie lost it, bursting into an adorable fit of laughter and apologizing as she tried to hold herself together.

"I'm so sorry." She hid her mouth behind her bouquet.

Sunny asked, "What's so funny?"

"Nothing," Cassie whispered. "Nothing," she repeated to the guests. "I'm so sorry."

Frankie continued the ceremony, and Cassie glared at Jake, her mouth combating a forming smile. He'd made Cassie laugh for the first time in years. He'd kissed her for the first and second time in years. He'd listened to her for the first time in years.

What would tonight bring if he acted on what was in his heart?

He needed Cassie a little more with each passing second.

He didn't prefer to die alone.

He didn't prefer to live his life alone, either.

Damn weddings.

****

For as special as the ceremony had been—full of hope and sap—he was back to the gut-punch-to-his-stomach feeling at the reception, located in an ivory tent on the far side of the Smith property.

The ground was grassy in most of the space, except for a slab of wood next to the live band. A group of old guys, who he recognized as The Crickets, played their instruments while people socialized. Matthew Smith had been The Crickets' banjo player before his passing.

A lump in his throat formed. His dad used to love playing music—a trait Missy had inherited as a pianist. He was thankful he'd found their dad's guitar pick in an old western book he'd taken with him when he left.

Missy seemed happy to have it now.

He kept to himself at his table, which also included his mom, Debbie Brooks and her husband, Frankie and Kate, and Parker's parents. The steak was excellent, but he could only eat half. He hadn't touched his potatoes, though that was less about nerves and more about the realization he'd be back on set in a couple days and would need to be fit enough to earn his paycheck. Every couple of minutes, people clanked their champagne glasses, and Missy and Parker kissed.

It was all fun and games until the newlyweds changed the rules. They asked their guests to write their names on strips of paper that Frankie distributed. He then collected them in a fishbowl. Every time the champagne flutes clinked for the rest of the night, Parker or Missy picked another person from the fishbowl who had to kiss his or her date.

Jake stuffed his slip of paper in his pocket. He had no one to kiss. Not publicly, anyway. Instead, he wiped his mouth with his napkin and excused himself to go to the bathroom. He needed a break from Frankie's attempts to be a brother, and Kate's nauseating display of love for him. Had he and Cassie ever displayed their relationship so openly? He'd done his best to avoid glancing at her throughout dinner, mostly so he could keep himself together before his brother-of-the-bride speech.

He took a couple extra seconds washing his hands. Weddings were awful for anyone without a date. Even for those who didn't want a partner on a daily basis. The reception was throwing him off the saddle. He'd known his role as his dad's replacement during the ceremony, but now he was fucking lost.

He took his time moving back to the reception tent.

"Hi, Jake."

The voice belonged to his cousin, Erin, who lived in Kansas as a kid, just like Dorothy from *The Wizard of Oz*. He was about to ask her what she was up to when he heard his name again—amplified. He turned toward the other end of the tent where a hundred set of eyes stared at him. Parker had the mic to his lips. It wasn't time for speeches yet, was it? His piss hadn't taken long. He glanced at the piece of paper in Parker's hand. The fishbowl was on the table.

Oh, hell no. Was this a setup or karma biting him in the ass?

Missy took the microphone from her new husband. "I actually think it's about time to start speeches. You want to head it up, Jake?"

He cleared his throat and glanced to the left of his sister where Cassie gently tucked her hair behind her ear. Her cheeks were red like she was embarrassed for him being called out publicly. Maybe she thought he'd charge the space and plant a sweet one on her. Part of him yearned to do it. Instead, he made his way to the front, stopping at the head table first to take the microphone from Missy, whom he hugged.

"Sorry," she whispered against his cheek. "I asked Frankie not to put your name in the bowl."

He eyed Frankie, who shrugged, glancing toward Cassie, and then back at him. He gave a thumbs-up. Deep down, Jake wasn't so mad at his brother's support of Cassandra Sullivan. It was just weird he was so interested.

Frankie's life must be boring these days.

Bringing the microphone to his lips, Jake's breath

sounded like Darth Vader's.

"Hollywood's gone to my head, apparently," he joked.

The crowd laughed. His hand gripped the table so hard that the wine glass in front of him shook.

"Just give me a minute." For the first time since his father had died, he prayed to him. *Give me the strength to say something meaningful, Dad.* He closed his eyes and waited. And waited. Every part of him ached as if he'd been thrown from a stunt. He was speaking at his baby sister's wedding, and he was too close to becoming a stereotypical blubbering idiot about it.

Breathe. He needed to fucking breathe.

He fisted his free hand at his side.

"It's hard for a man to know what to say when his sister has always been the smarter one, especially regarding love." He turned toward Missy and Parker, who were leaning into each other like their love was a revealed secret everyone in the room got to witness. More emotion balled up in his throat.

"Just never stop caring enough to say what needs to be said when it needs to be said, do what needs to be done when it needs to be done, and cherishing the moments that seem ordinary."

He paused.

He'd shared many ordinary moments with Cassie—kissing her in the kitchen and hoping his dad wouldn't catch them. Or worse, his mom. Attempting to teach Cassie to lasso. She'd ended up looping the rope around him, and maybe that had been what she'd intended all along. More kisses. More time spent together.

His head instantly hurt.

He wouldn't break down in front of everyone. He goddamn refused to. Lovestruck had enough to talk about when it came to "Jacob Smith" as a subject.

"Those people who can take the simple tasks of sharing coffee in the morning or doing chores on a Sunday afternoon, and in those moments say, 'this is the life. We've made it.' Those are the people I admire. Those are the people I know you two will turn out to be. I love you, Missy. Parker, you're a good man. Here's to your shared future." He raised his glass. "And here's to as many ordinary days as possible." He stared at Cassie. "I promise to be part of them from now on."

He needed her to hear his words—to understand he was going to make an effort at mending what he could for the sake of being able to come back to Lovestruck from time-to-time.

People clapped and whistled. Cassie wiped a tear from her cheek. How many tears had he caused her since he'd left? Probably not as many as if he'd stayed. That was the kick in the ass he avoided thinking about. He had no idea how to make Cassie happy anymore, as evidenced by her constant annoyance this weekend.

He accepted the nagging feeling, however, that he was willing to relearn everything. He didn't deserve half of what she'd given him this weekend by talking to him. Cassie had let him touch her. Kiss her. Marvel at her.

He was the luckiest chap in the world.

He sat down and speeches continued. He barely survived Cassie's as she talked about the sister Missy had become for her—their status as soulmates and sometimes bedmates when Missy visited; the blessing Missy was in Cassie's life. It was like listening to a highlight reel of everything he'd missed out on for seven years.

The Crickets played Missy and Parker's first song, a Johnny Cash tune, which brought everyone's attention to the dance floor. The party music started afterward. Sunny skipped to his mom, and he smiled at the bond between the two. What kid wouldn't like Bridget Smith? She was known as the town's mother. And now, the town's grandmother.

"Will you get more cake with me?" Sunny asked.

"Of course, my sunshine," his mom answered.

"Not too much." .

His mom and Sunny looked at each other as they walked hand-in-hand. They were trouble together. Jake attempted his own version of trouble. Cassie licked her lips when he leaned across the table and whispered, "I can't stop looking at you."

She took her sipping straw from her drink and played with it. "That's just because I'm right here, Jake. Give it two days when you're home again."

He let the jab slide. He stood, and Cassie glared at his movements until he crouched down behind her, speaking into her ear. Her back straightened at his proximity.

"You know, they say people who fidget are sexually frustrated," he whispered.

He hoped the more he made light of their shared lust for each other, the more successful he might be in getting another chance alone with her. He needed to remind her that she didn't always want to slug him.

It was a wedding, for Christ's sake. People were supposed to be in good moods.

She dropped her straw back into her drink.

"I'm not sexually frustrated." Cassie bit her lip.

"Would it help you admit it if I said I am, too?"

She turned toward him only a fraction. "You're crazy."

"Maybe."

Frankie approached the table. "You two talking about mending fences or what?" He stared at her, and she moved her weight on her chair.

"Jake was just propositioning—"

"I was asking Cass to dance." He stood, only slightly defeated. He was working toward a horizontal situation with her, but a slow dance may help his case. *Dirty Dancing* was a classic for a reason. Missy had made him watch it repeatedly growing up. "Hungry Eyes" still got stuck in his head sometimes. He just needed to be close to Cassie.

He extended his hand, palm up, to her. His skin was clammy.

She stared at Jake's fingers and then at him, taking her sweet, torturous time to reach his face. He could sense with *every bone* in his body that she wanted him. And she could have him—no conversation attached—if she'd say yes to it.

She stood.

"Okay, let's dance." She bumped his shoulder as she walked toward the dance floor, refusing to take his hand. He chuckled. His lady was independent as ever, and he adored it. Hell, he'd always loved her independence, despite the quality also being a pain in his ass.

She smiled small at Frankie, mouthing something. Jake didn't know what. Nor did he care.

The music was mid-tempo, but he still grabbed

Cassie's waist and pulled her against his chest as he led her hands to a slow dance position. She didn't make a fool of him by pushing away. Instead, Cassie rested her palms in his and let him guide her along the busy dance floor. Their bodies never lost contact.

"People are staring," Cassie said.

"Maybe not for reasons you think. You're the prettiest woman here, Cassie. People are going to stare."

She rested her forehead on his chest and laughed.

"What?"

"You're impossible."

"Impossibly charming?"

"Jake." She shook her head against his shirt. When she stared at him again, her eyes were dilated. She squeezed his hand and then let go.

"Cass." The lack of contact physically hurt.

"Meet me at my house in fifteen minutes."

His forehead pinched.

"You heard me, cowboy. We're going to talk. Alone." She folded her arms, and stepped away, bumping directly into his mom.

He covered his mouth, chuckling.

"Where are you running off to, dear?" his mom held Sunny's hand as the little girl urged her to dance, yanking, pleading.

Cassie touched her forehead, which seemed to inspire an excuse. "My head. My head hurts. I'm going to lie down for a little while. Could you keep an eye on Sunny for me?"

She pinched Sunny's cheek. "Be good for Bridg-Bridg and don't go anywhere without telling her."

His mom watched, along with Jake, as Cassie left.

She was already staring at him when he turned toward her.

"What?" He cleared his throat. "Stop looking at me like that."

She smiled, nearly losing balance when Sunny yanked her again.

"Bridg-Bridg," the little girl whined.

"Are you going to have a headache in fifteen minutes, too?"

"I'm going to get a soda." He pushed past dancing couples and away from his ever-the-wise-one mother.

Fifteen minutes. He had fifteen minutes to survive.

"Jake-y," Norma sing-songed, pinching his ass.

He was literally going to go nuts.

Chapter Fourteen

Cassie

Jake's speech had been simple and beautiful. Her heart both broke and filled with nostalgia at his sentiments. She dreamed of ordinary moments, too. Lovestruck allotted her many of those types of memories—picnics, long walks, and family dinners filled with laughter. But she also dreamed of the extraordinary in her life—those days that bloomed like the prettiest flowers. Which was why she'd asked Jake to meet her in fifteen minutes.

Jake was extraordinary.

She needed to talk to him.

But she shouldn't.

She should.

It was after the wedding. She didn't have to worry about any family members getting mad at her timing.

No, she shouldn't say anything.

Yes, she should.

No, it could ruin everything.

Yes, but if it went well, it could fix some things.

Her thoughts sounded like "he loves me, he loves me not," a game she'd played many nights about the same man. Was he worth this trouble? This insanity?

Cassie stared at the clock—an antique grandfather fixture in her living room. It was dark and had a brassy tongue. Forty-two minutes had passed, and Jake still wasn't at her doorstep. She paced in the foyer until she heard his heavy footsteps on her porch.

"Come in," she called when he pulled the screen open and rapped on the door.

She used the railing for support when she saw him. He hadn't run away or decided against coming. Frankie hadn't gotten a hold of him before her. Jake was here, and the time for truth was now.

Truth number one: He was miserably handsome. His suit and hair were slightly ruffled after today. Total perfection. His Adam's apple bobbed and, dammit, if even his gulping didn't do something for her. She wanted to trail kisses all over his neck.

Outside, the dusty purple sky and the Christmas lights she'd put on the trees for more lighting, made Jake's shadow bigger. Bolder. Scarier as he stood in the doorway.

"Sorry it took me a little longer to get here," he said.

"Me, too."

He seemed to understand her answer because he nodded.

Her body ached for him—a poetic, inspired ache that burned inside her. During his speech, he'd said he would be part of more Smith family memories. What did that mean? Because if he were to suddenly show up at things, it was yet another reason he needed the truth. They needed this moment.

"Frankie wanted to talk," he explained. "And before that, Norma got in a good pinch on my ass."

Her heart quickened. She attempted to sound breezy. "What did Frankie want to talk about?"

Jake took off his cowboy hat and put it on a hook by the door. "Me, actually. He was asking how I liked working in Hollywood. He was weird about it though." Jake chuckled. "Maybe he's jealous. He asked a lot of questions about my five-year plan."

"Los Angeles does have a different flair than the east coast," she answered. "It's like a unicorn."

Jake shrugged. "The town pays well, and the life isn't bad."

His words were arrogant, but his tone wasn't. He truly was a man who believed if a person worked hard, success would follow. She stepped toward him and when she was arm's length, he pulled her to his chest in a different dance altogether.

He gazed at her.

"All the years gone by," he said simply. "I still like having you in my arms, despite your ability to frustrate the hell out of me."

"Yeah." She bit her lower lip.

His stare flicked to her mouth.

"Can I kiss you, Cassie?"

Talk, her thoughts screamed.

"We've already kissed." Her voice was airy, and her body was all sensation. Fidgety and heated. Her lower belly ached.

"And that's why I want to do it again. If you want to."

The vulnerability in his voice convinced her doubts to believe that touching him was okay.

"What do you need to talk about?" His lips grazed her cheek.

To be wanted—truly wanted by another human— was more powerful than anything she'd ever experienced. Jake wasn't her weakness on all fronts. He made her proud of herself. Someone as good as him cared about her.

"So much." She wrapped her arms around his neck.

He pressed his lips to hers.

He tasted like soda and cinnamon. Jake lifted one of her legs around his waist. She hopped up and wrapped her other leg around him. He was steady. Strong. Safe. Somehow, they made it to her bedroom upstairs. How hadn't she heard the stomping of his feet or the sound of his grunts as he carried her?

Jake was a magician.

Or a stuntman.

The fact that his life was not in Lovestruck made her pull away, but then Jake's mouth was back on her—worshipping her.

Who wouldn't want to be worshipped?

"End of the hallway." Cassie nearly begged.

He smiled against her neck. "I know where I'm going."

She laughed, her lips on his temple. Of course he knew. This house was where they'd slept together for the first time as a younger Cassie and a younger Jake. They'd known the foreman was out of town at his girlfriend's apartment, and they'd snuck in to christen the guest bedroom downstairs.

Now, this was her house, and Jake was stumbling into her bedroom on the second floor—a wood-floored space with a bed and a vanity. It was rustic, with accents of blue, purple, and green. A big oak dresser took the place of a walk-in closet.

Jake laid her onto the mattress and stood above her, looking every bit the Brad Pitt cowboy fantasy he was.

Even in his suit, he was more rugged than tailored. He discarded his coat and placed it on a lilac chair near the vanity she used on the rare occasions when she dressed up.

He stared at his reflection in the mirror.

"What?" She propped herself on one elbow.

"I can't believe we're doing this."

He turned, sauntered over, and placed a knee on the bed. Slowly, he loosened his tie and pulled it off, tossing it aside. He played with the first three buttons of his shirt, undoing them delicately. His stare stayed on her, and she squirmed against her sheets as she laid down, wanting everything from him all at once. Still, she loved the time he was taking for this moment. He wasn't rushing. He wasn't running away.

She was hot as fire, but the flames weren't spreading fast enough. *To hell with his sweetness.*

"Too slow." She crawled to him and unbuttoned the rest of his shirt, gliding her fingers up his chest which had just enough hair to make it a roughened journey. When she reached his shoulders, she guided his shirt off him. His skin was warm and darker in the dim room. He'd gotten a tattoo on his mid-ribs during his time away from Lovestruck.

It was a horseshoe.

Her finger traced it as he watched, gripping her shoulders. He breathed erratically—the only hint, besides the bulge in his pants—that he wanted her as badly as she wanted him. Maybe his want was more of a need, too.

Maybe she'd ask him eventually.

She had all but decided they had to talk by the time he showed up tonight. What a dumb idea that was.

Her hands moved from his torso to his neck to his hair. She tugged at his locks; thankful he was real. And that he hadn't gotten his hair cut. Many a night she'd woken to her hands in the air trying to grasp for him, but he was gone. Now, he wasn't.

His stare met hers, and he whispered, "You're beautiful."

"Jake." Her hands fell to his waistband. She yanked.

"You're going to rip my pants," he mocked, kicking them off the rest of the way.

She loved the huskiness of his voice, and the need in his tone matched the need in her heart. It always had. She feared it always would.

"You have too many clothes on as well, sassy Cassie." He crawled backward to watch as she unzipped her dress and slid it off of her body irreverently. She threw it somewhere over her shoulder.

"I'm excited, too."

"Shut up." She laid down. Her head fell against her pillow, even as her gaze stayed on him. He lowered his head to her leg.

"God." She groaned as he kissed her ankle.

"God's not here." He trailed kisses up each of her shins.

She fisted the sheets. "Jake, please."

He stopped his kisses at her hips and rose, his knees on either side of her stomach. His hands glided to her breasts, palming them delicately.

She trailed her fingertips against his cheek.

"Condom," he asked.

"IUD."

"I haven't been with anyone in a long time." He

lowered his mouth to her lips and repositioned his body over hers. The heat between them was hotter than the sun. As they kissed, she brought her hands down, attempting to guide him inside her. They were close but not close enough.

She tilted her pelvis upward, and he slid in—a little at first. She shuddered. He swore, resting his forehead on hers. He lifted his lips and kissed her.

"Cassie." Her name was a plea.

She slinked her arms around his upper back and brought her heels to his impressively hard ass, pushing him deeper.

He took over, setting the rhythm, which she matched thrust for thrust. The sound of their skin together was the applause confirming this was right.

They were right.

They would always be all right.

The perfect conversation.

Her soft moans and his irreverent grunts blended with the ceiling fan. She stared at him and gripped his sturdy, threaded forearms on either side of her head.

His gaze roamed from her eyes to her lips, where he leaned down to press the most beautiful fib against her mouth. "You're perfect."

"I've missed you."

"You feel so good."

"Jake," she whimpered as his mouth trailed to her shoulder, nibbling. He pressed his forehead against her neck and continued to move inside her.

"Let go, Cass." Her name in his raspy voice sounded like an old blues lyric. Her chest pushed toward him, and her back arched as she tipped her head against the pillow, letting out a sound she didn't recognize. Her grip loosened on his arms, and her palms smacked the mattress.

"Yes," she moaned. "Jake, yes."

He lifted his head from her shoulder and kissed her. She swallowed every small growl he gave as his pace sped.

"So good," he groaned against her tongue. He moved three more times and met his own oblivion. A couple seconds later, he fell onto his forearms and breathed against her neck. She kissed his temple, savoring his weight against her until he rolled to his side and tucked her against his torso.

She clung onto his arms long after they'd settled into reality.

His fingertips glided across her bare belly, spreading goosebumps in their wake. Their breaths, fast and spent, filled the room with the type of love she'd hoped for since he left.

The Jake Smith style of loving.

Each struggling puff of air, she questioned, *What does this mean?*

Each struggling puff of air, she hoped he was answering, *Whatever we want it to.*

****

In the kitchen, she took her time sipping from her mug of coffee. She'd redressed in Jake's button-up shirt and her own pajama pants, even though she'd have to slip into her dress again if she returned to the reception. She didn't particularly want to miss Parker and Missy riding out on Caramel. She'd also eventually need to pick up Sunny.

She hadn't lied when she'd told Bridget she had a headache. Resting wasn't her cure of choice, however.

As she reminisced on the healing effects of Jake's manhood, Sunny skipped in through the front door. She heard Jake greet her daughter at the staircase along with Frankie and Kate.

"You okay?" Frankie asked Cassie from the kitchen doorway. She gazed at him, her eyes and head still fuzzy from intimacy. She imagined her hair was pure frizz.

"What?" she asked, as if awaking from a dream.

"Sunny was tired, so I told Mom I'd bring her back here. I didn't know Jake came, too."

Cassie's cheeks warmed at his word choice.

"Did you guys talk?"

She timidly shook her head.

"Damn, Cassie." Frankie pulled out a dollar and put it into Sunny's curse jar by the refrigerator. "You promised you'd talk to him when he was here this weekend." He pointed at her post-sex glow. "Presumably before you did this. Kate and I are getting antsy."

'Kate and I' was salt in the wound—like they were on a team she wasn't. She didn't belong anywhere in her own life. Three's damn company.

"Talk to me about what?" Jake walked around his brother to sit at Cassie's kitchen table as if he owned the place. He had put on an oversized sweatshirt he must have retrieved from her dresser along with his crinkled dress pants. He scanned through the same pile of papers and envelopes in front of him from his earlier visit.

"How badly is the dude ranch doing?" He thumbed through the first document. "Is that why you're thinking about selling it? A money thing?"

"It's not the only reason." When Cassie's mother stopped sending her money, she no longer had the supplemental income to help pay off monthly shortfalls and pursue her other interests. But now there was the job opportunity in New York—the type of job she would've gotten had she followed the path laid out for her before Sunny.

She didn't need to explain herself.

"You've decided that part of my life is none of your business." She slapped his hand away, gathered the papers, and disappeared into her office. When she returned, Jake and Frankie were talking about the project Jake was contracted to start next week in California. Another sore subject—his departure. Her mood deflated into a wallowing mess of self-pity.

"I'm nervous about it," Jake said uncharacteristically. "I fell out of a moving train car on my last job." His tone was formal toward Frankie. Distant. But cordial enough.

This was progress.

His hair was messier than usual, compliments of her gripping it. Currently, Cassie was tempted to tear at her own locks. There were too many secrets in this room.

Kate walked down the stairs, wiping her damp hands on her dress. "Sunny wants you to tuck her in. She was talking to herself when I passed her door to use your bathroom."

"Okay." Cassie eyed Jake for a beat before turning to Frankie. "Do you guys want to stay, and I'll be right down to talk?"

She bit her lip as she looked at Frankie earnestly.

"Sure," Frankie answered, a knowing tone in his

voice.

Jake's gaze moved from Kate to Cassie. As for Cassie, she was mortified at the spectacle. She was wearing Jake's shirt with her baby daddy and Kate in her kitchen while her child was upstairs, and while Jake was shining in his post-sex glow.

So the Greek mythology thing she was trying to avoid? She'd failed miserably.

She moved quickly to the staircase in the foyer. Her heart raced from more than the mind-blowing sex she'd experienced with the only man who could gift her with it. How could she care about two men in such different ways? After not getting married, thank God, she and Frankie had become friends eventually. He now sent her money every month for their daughter. When he could afford to, he also sent extra for the ranch. He made a good living, but it wasn't enough to support two households.

And Jake was Jake.

She cared about him in a way that wasn't defined solely in who he was, but in who she was in his eyes. He may not believe it anymore, but Jake used to tell her she could rule the world if she wanted to. He'd treated her like she could do anything. Like they could be anything together.

"Mommy!"

"Coming, honey." Cassie turned toward the stairs.

She wished to bask in her post-horizontal-dance glow for a little longer. Still, she had to have a civil conversation about the day that changed all of their lives. Jake had already made it known he was leaving after this weekend. Despite sleeping together, their hearts were in different places. Sure, he'd come around more, but an actual long-distance relationship was impossible. Especially if she ended up in New York.

More fashion. More creating. Her heart yearned to make a move finally.

"But I don't want to lose him," she whispered in the hallway. To say that aloud was powerful. Like since she'd named what was hurting her, it lost some of its effect. She'd never wanted to lose Jake. That didn't mean much regarding whatever was going to happen. She had no control over the outcome. She surrendered to the bed she'd made.

Chapter Fifteen

Jake

Jake rode the pony of post-sex satisfaction—so much so that he almost hadn't caught onto the awkwardness looming in Cassie's house since Frankie had arrived. Had it been there every time Cassie and his brother interacted?

Even odder, Frankie was being too nice to him this weekend. Sure, they'd had the moment in the kitchen where their mom had to intervene, but Jake had to admit—likely because of his recent Cassie-induced orgasm—he'd been a big part to blame for that particular tiff.

He sat across the table from Frankie now.

"And how's life for you?" The words sounded strained coming out of his mouth.

Frankie took an apple from Cassie's fruit bowl in the middle of the table. He set it down and rolled it between his hands.

"Business is good," Frankie said. "It's a seller's market for Cassie when—" He stopped the apple.

"I told you I know she's thinking about selling the land," Jake said.

"She's more than thinking about it."

Jake nodded. "I heard you guys while I was showering. You didn't want to tell me something until after the wedding. I imagine you were trying to spare my feelings since this place used to mean so much to me."

"Spare your feelings about land?" Frankie said slowly.

"Land means something to some people," Jake argued. He closed his eyes as a dozen memories of his time ranching.

Kate, who, had been in the bathroom again, walked into the kitchen. She kissed Frankie's forehead as she rested her hand on his shoulder.

"I have to retire for the night," she said.

Frankie patted her hand. "I'll be there shortly."

Kate glanced at Jake. "It was nice meeting you this weekend."

Jake opened his eyes. "You, too."

Frankie focused on the door even after his wife left. Had Cassie done the same thing after Jake had fled Lovestruck? Would she this time?

He tapped his knuckles against the table. "Easy there, big bro. Kate will be in your tent when you go back."

"I'm a blessed man for it. She's way out of my league, but somehow she tolerates me." Frankie smiled.

In any other world, the man sitting across from Jake wouldn't have bothered him. Frankie was charming in the same way Jake was a grade-A stick in the mud. Maybe Jake was jealous of the fact Frankie seemed happy with the path he'd chosen in life. Meanwhile, he was still on the bull and trying not to get bucked off.

"I don't hate you," Jake admitted. This confession was a good enough place to start. He looked around the kitchen, so he didn't have to take in Frankie's widening smile. Cassie's home was tidy but lived in, with appliances lining her countertop.

"You'd have reason to hate me, Jakey-boy. I just hope we can be friends at some point."

Jake nodded once as he made his way to the cupboard for a glass. He'd helped Cassie get the mugs down earlier, so he remembered where she kept them.

"You can start by calling me Jake." His back was to Frankie.

"Jake," Frankie corrected. "You used to like it when I called you Jakey-boy. I didn't know it bothered you now."

He rubbed a hand over his face. He'd forgotten he had once enjoyed the nickname. God only knew why. There was another long silence before Frankie interrupted it.

"I don't hate you, either."

Jake filled his glass with water and approached his chair again.

Frankie frowned.

"What? Do you want one?"

"You did that very easily," Frankie said.

He rolled his eyes. "I got water. I didn't move all my clothes in."

"I don't want you getting too comfortable. Seven years is a long time and a lot happens to people. You guys rolling in the hay hasn't changed that."

"It wasn't hay. Despite your thinking I'm a lesser person than you, I do my business in beds." However, a roll in the hay wasn't out of the question. But who the hell was Frankie to pontificate? Or judge?

Jake redirected the conversation. "Like I said, I

understand that Cassie's selling the land. I'm in no position to stop her."

Frankie paused. "Cassie has a potential job opportunity in New York, and it sounds like she might actually take an interview."

"Would she ever move far from Lovestruck?" Jake hadn't anticipated this part of her decision. His conversation with Mr. Karl no longer made sense. Cassie wasn't taking over I Do Boutique. Why had the idea that she was staying in town make his shoulders relax? He would've paid to have her hightail it away from Lovestruck forty-eight hours ago.

He was confused because of sex. It was the only explanation. Well, the only one he'd accept.

"We've all left, Jake," Frankie answered. "If Cassie has an opportunity, she should take it if she wants to. She'll be closer to Kate and me, and with the kids now—"

"Kids?"

Frankie smiled like a Cheshire cat. "Kate's pregnant."

"Wow." Frankie was going to be a dad before him. Jake resented this awful fact. Nothing in his life had gone the way he'd imagined. He was bitter at his dad for dying, and he was angry at himself for not being able to handle it. Everyone's life seemed to be moving forward—or at least moving—while his was stagnant. His body slumped—every part of him hurt.

"Congratulations." Jake took another drink. "Does Mom know?"

"About which part?"

"All of it. This is a lot of shit you unloaded."

"Good shit," Frankie added.

That was a matter of perspective.

"Kate and I were waiting until after the wedding to say anything about the baby," Frankie said. "And as far as I know, Cassie was going to talk to Mom about the job when she'd decided for sure."

"Well, that's swell," Jake said. He'd seriously believed Cassie would still be around Lovestruck to keep an eye on the land, even if she didn't own it anymore. He thought she'd work on fashion *in town*. The market here was dense since I Do was the only bridal and formal wear shop in three counties. Did this new information change his view on the potential sale of the property?

"Mom is going to be devastated if Cassie leaves."

Frankie shook his head. "Come on. You have more to say than how Mom is going to feel."

He ran his hand through his hair. Enough of the gel from the morning was gone, so his fingers slid easily. "I don't like the idea of the family land getting sold to an outside buyer."

"It's not up to you," Frankie answered.

"I know, Frankie."

"Do you? Do you actually understand how much Cassie went through to keep it all this time?" Frankie's words were accusatory. Or they felt that way, at least. "Dammit. You don't get it at all."

"Where are you going?" Jake asked, chugging the rest of his water as Frankie stood. He put the glass down loudly, even though he hadn't intended to. Everything he did was heavy this weekend.

"Just going to take a piss." He patted Jake's shoulder as he walked around the table. "Glad to know you'll miss me."

Jake merely chuckled.

As he sat alone at the kitchen table, twiddling his thumbs, he exhaled. Could he really let Cassie sell the land to just any old schmuck? This was worse than his leaving seven years ago. He was ignorant to what happened then. Up until a couple months ago, he'd figured his mom had sold the land off already, and not to Cassie. Ignorance was bliss.

Now he was out of control.

He got up, plodding to the office, once the guest room, where Cassie had put the stack of mail he'd snooped through earlier. Maybe there was information about what she was thinking of doing or how behind she was on payments. He could help her somehow or give her his opinion on potential buyers.

He reached into the cupboard, and a card fell to his feet.

"Shit." He bent down to retrieve the opened paper. His heartbeat pounded as he read the note at the bottom of it. It was from Sunny's father, who had a familiar name—too familiar—if the envelope that accompanied it was true.

It couldn't be true.

It was impossible.

Except it wasn't.

It was written in bold, black letters.

A truth he couldn't unlearn.

The ground beneath him rumbled like a herd of cattle coming at him. He held onto the desk chair and growled. "What the fuck?"

Frankie was Sunny's dad.

Chapter Sixteen

Cassie

"And they lived—"

"What the fuck?" Jake's voice was a dull boom downstairs.

Cassie stared at Sunny, sleeping against her chest, her arms wrapped around her waist. This precious little girl was not the reason for the forthcoming fight, and Cassie would hurt both men downstairs if her Sunny heard any of this.

"Those boys couldn't have waited three more minutes," she mumbled. Cassie had intercepted every interaction the brothers had—at the kitchen table, at the rehearsal dinner, and at the wedding—so Frankie wouldn't slip up. A short bedtime story shouldn't have been a problem, especially when Kate was with them. From their previous conversation, Kate had understood Cassie wanted to tell Jake this weekend. The truth was always meant to come from her and her alone.

They'd decided this well before the cowboy downstairs had arrived in Lovestruck, dammit.

She tucked the powder blue sheets around Sunny and kissed her forehead, grateful her child slept through most noises. Oddly enough, only the sound of rain woke her daughter. Not the thundering downstairs.

Cassie took the steps two at a time. She second

guessed the ease she'd found moments ago about getting caught. Jake sounded downright pissed. Sex had not subdued him. This time, it was she who yearned to run away.

But she couldn't.

And she wouldn't.

They weren't fighting over a child but over a pregnancy; not over a love triangle but over a perverse coincidence. Enough time had passed, and everyone needed to grow up. Still, her memories with Jake flashed before her eyes—vignettes through rose-colored glasses. She slipped at the bottom of the stairs but pushed forward, toward the noise, clutching her stomach. She was still in Jake's shirt.

Her office stored many memories. It was the ranch hand's old guest room where she and Jake had made love more than once seven years ago.

Now, Jake stood near her desk, shaking an envelope at Frankie.

The brothers turned when she was in the doorway.

Jake was where the guest bed had been—the one they'd kissed on as younger adults. Her memories raced back to when he'd tripped over the foreman's shoes, and they'd both fumbled onto the mattress, laughing against each other's mouths while they pulled at each other's clothing.

"Cassie," Jake interrupted her sex-of-times-past thoughts.

"Yeah." She shook her head and glanced around the room. "Where's Kate?"

Her hands trembled, and her heart pounded. She was in survival mode. This time, she was going to fight.

"Kate went back to our tent. She was tired,"

Frankie said. "And Jake found my card to Sunny while I was in the bathroom."

"I see." They exchanged sympathetic smiles.

"Don't look at her like that," Jake said.

"Shut up," Frankie answered.

She held up her hand. "Jake, you gave up the right to care about how anyone looks at me a long time ago." She crossed her arms, attempting strength and defiance. Who was he to snoop? Of course, she was making up reasons to be angry. She was still formulating her explanation. "Opening another person's mail is a felony or a crime or...something."

She needed to watch more crime shows.

"What is this?" Stepping closer, he pointed to the top left corner. "What is this envelope with my brother's address on it and a wad of cash? Tell me Frankie has a high debt to be paid off for his cursing when he visits."

"That's not yours, Jake."

"Let's see whose it is, shall we." He opened the card, though he'd clearly already read it. "A girl like you is worth all the sunshine in the world. I love you, Sunny. See you soon. Love, Dad."

He slammed the card shut dramatically. His breathing was heavy. He resembled an animal.

"What is this?" he repeated.

She ached unexpectedly for him.

"The truth," she whispered.

The truth shall set hell free.

"You've got to be shitting me." Jake's voice cracked.

"You left before I could tell you." She remained calm, hoping it would temper him instead of spur his anger.

"You cheated on me?" His eyes were wide—wild.

"No," she answered defiantly. He had no excuse, except for her timing, to get angry. Not anymore. He'd made choices, too.

"When did this happen?" He turned toward his brother. "How could this have happened? You were only in Lovestruck for two weeks the whole summer, Frankie. Did you swoop in after I left?"

Frankie rubbed the back of his neck. "It happened before you two met."

"What?" Jake seethed.

She braced against the doorframe. "Your brother and I were at Lushes the night before he had his farewell dinner."

"You were supposed to be there, too, Jake. You ended up working late at the ranch."

"Are you blaming me for not showing up?" Jake argued.

"No, man. I'm explaining." Frankie stared out the window. "It was just one of those things that happened."

Cassie added, "We're friends now, Jake. But we're nothing more."

"Not anymore," Frankie muttered.

"Cheese and rice." She covered her forehead. Men were idiots. Even ones who were being honest. Frankie's tact was nonexistent, which was saying something about a man in the financial industry.

"What does that mean?" Jake looked between Cassie and Frankie.

She cursed under her breath. They had to keep spiraling down the rabbit hole. "Frankie and I almost got married."

Jake groaned, closing his eyes and pinching the bridge of his nose. His other hand fisted at his side. "What?"

Frankie cleared his throat. "We were at the courthouse in Boston and—"

"Franklin." She stopped him. "He gets the point. Stop sharing the wrong details."

Jake moved toward the door.

"Wait," she pleaded. "We couldn't follow through with something that neither of us believed in. I was heartbroken after you left. I was looking for stability. For family. I went to Boston a month after Matthew's funeral to tell Frankie about my pregnancy, and we tried to do what we thought was right. I wanted a family."

"With him?" Jake pointed at Frankie like he was a toothless troll.

She scowled. "Frankie is becoming a good father, Jake. Loving. Supportive. It's you who disappeared from *my* life. You who were my lover and my friend. But my situation wasn't your mess. I was confused. I didn't even like Frankie on our wedding day, and I didn't want to stay on the east coast with him. We weren't even together. We never have been. It was so screwed up."

"That's true." Frankie chimed in, rubbing his jaw line. "We aren't meant for even friendship. But I wanted to do what I thought I should. Dad had just died. Cassie was freaking out about the pregnancy. I was freaking out. I'd just gotten into my business program, for Christ's sake. You left Lovestruck before she could tell you, so she left, too. We had to do something. We went to the courthouse, and I finally talked sense into both of us. Family doesn't have to look conventional."

Cassie nodded. "I left for those couple of months after you did, Jake. I went to see my dad when Frankie and I parted ways, but he had all but washed his hands clean of the drama relating to our family. He tried. He really tried. I had no place to go. Lovestruck saved my life. Your family, Jake. They saved my life."."

The memories still took her breath away.

When she was ready, she continued. "I came back here heavily pregnant, and people assumed that I'd had a good time somewhere else. Of course there were other rumors about you and me, but the general consensus was that my baby wasn't yours. You would've never left me if Sunny was yours."

"Is that little sob story supposed to make me feel better?" Jake spit the words at her.

"No, Jacob. The truth is I hated that you left and never came back. But I also hated myself because I didn't know how to explain to you what happened even if you did return. It was better you stayed away. It was easier. You didn't fit into the puzzle anymore."

He gritted his teeth. "Just like now?"

She lowered her head. "It's turning out that way."

"What other way is there?" He sounded exasperated. "You seriously believe I'd sleep with you tonight, and it would be enough to get over this? Was that your plan?"

"No."

"Do people know now that Frankie is Sunny's dad? Have I been pitied all weekend?"

She cleared her throat. "Frankie being in town

more consistently makes sense, given the rumors about my selling the property eventually. Plus, Bridget's getting older, and he wants Kate and his kids to know her. I think most people believe he's stepping in for you around the ranch. No one asks me directly. I mean, Sunny has started calling him 'dad' occasionally, but we haven't been in town when she does. She's only begun to understand that Frankie's her father because in her little world of friends, no one's dad lives far away. It's still a process for her." She exhaled. "I'm so sorry."

It didn't feel like enough to apologize, but what else could she say?

That she loved Jake?

That she'd always loved him?

That it wasn't possible, but if it was, she ached for Sunny to be Jake's child?

She remembered her conversation with Bridget. She absolutely should admit all those words, but she didn't want to confess them to make him stay or so he'd forgive her. She couldn't speak the truth in desperate hopes he'd play softball with Sunny in the morning. She yearned for her words to be said and felt without complication. Problem was, she and Jake would never be a simple love story, and it was her fault more than his.

"I'm so sorry," she repeated, wishing those weren't the only three words she had for him.

Chapter Seventeen

Jake

"You're so sorry?" Jake couldn't take this. His veins tightened even as his blood rushed, and his head hurt. His body ached. He saw red. The kind of red a bull saw when a cape mocked him.

He approached his brother, who stood quietly in the foul stink of his truth.

Jake punched him.

He'd wanted to do it for the past five minutes. Actually, he'd wanted to do it half his life. Fist to jaw. Fist to cheek. Frankie had been trying to be a brother this weekend, and for a second before this conversation, Jake actually believed his effort was authentic.

But no.

Frankie was a dick.

He'd slept with Cassie. If that wasn't disrespect with a cherry on top, he didn't know what was. The timing of their indiscretion didn't matter. It had happened. And no one said a goddamn word until now.

"Jake." Cassie grabbed his arm as she checked to see if Frankie was all right.

"He's fine."

Frankie grumbled. "I'm not fine, Jake."

The pain in Frankie's voice tore at him only a little.

He settled his breaths. Cassie's concern for Frankie

only made him ready to punch his brother again. What in the devil's name was this shitshow?

"I did everything right with you, and he got the family," Jake yelled.

"You did everything right?" Cassie half-laughed, half-chided.

He threw up his hands. "I did. I loved you."

"Jake, you left." Her voice was firm.

"And I explained why."

"When?" Frankie mumbled.

Cassie waved him off. Her voice was low, raspy, and direct when she said, "If you wanted a family with me so bad, you would have let me in after your dad died. You shut me out completely. That's not love."

"You didn't press hard enough. That's not love, either." Jake needed to destroy something. "What was I supposed to think when you wouldn't say 'I love you' even after my dad passed?" Those last two words still got stuck in his throat every damn time he said them. Always surreal. Always a blow to the balls.

This moment didn't feel much different.

"Now you know why I didn't," she answered. "I was a little busy with another life-altering event." Tears filled her eyes. "I couldn't tell you I loved you, and then in the next sentence tell you I was pregnant with your brother's baby. You wouldn't have believed me. I hardly knew what I was doing those dark days. But my feelings for you were always true, and it kills me knowing you never got to hear them. You were my world, and just like you, I lost everything that summer."

He opened his mouth, but not one damn thing came out.

"I'm going to grab a pack of peas and get out of

here, if you're okay, Cassandra." Frankie rubbed the already black-and-blue flesh on his cheek.

"I'm fine. We're fine," Cassie answered.

"We aren't a 'we.'"

She rolled her eyes. "You're being an asshole, Jake."

Frankie stared at him. "I'm sorry I hurt you, Jake, but try to remember I wasn't the reason you two didn't work out. You didn't know about Sunny until this weekend. You played the jackass in your life all by yourself. I've owned the hurt I didn't mean to cause. It's your turn now."

He left with that hell of a mic drop, and Jake almost clapped, if the truth wasn't so pointed at him.

His fingers twitched with the desire to touch her, to hold her and find his comfort in her. No other part of him supported his desire. For once, logic reigned. His chest pounded. Bile rose in his throat. He moved toward the waste basket beside the desk, and coughed up grief, loss, and regret.

He turned to her afterward.

She'd been watching him with crossed arms. She wasn't defiant. She was staring, her eyes brimming with unfallen tears.

He wiped his mouth.

An eerie silence fell between them when Frankie left; the type that came after a tornado tore through, and people emerged from their basements to assess the damage.

Jake slumped into her desk chair.

Cassie backstepped to rest against the doorframe.

How many people ended up at the same rock bottom—frozen in place—waiting for someone to break the cold war, if only to ask, *how did we hit this bottom?*

They had sex a couple hours ago.

"I'm going to change," she finally said. "We can talk after if you want."

He ran his hand over his face. He wanted to talk, but not to Cassie. The clock on her desk read three in the morning. How had a couple hours passed in silence? Apparently, time flew just as fast when a person wasn't having fun.

"I don't think it's a good idea right now, Cass."

"Of course not." She shook her head. "Why should I expect anything different from you?"

She should expect more, but this time, it wasn't like that. He needed space, and his mommy.

"Do you know where my mom would be right now?"

"She lives in Gayle Frita's old place."

He hated he didn't know that. He stood and straightened his pants.

"My shirt." He inclined his head toward her.

She slipped his shirt over her head, covering her breasts with her arm as she handed him his top.

They'd taken a million steps backward.

"Cassie, I can wait for you to change." His tone softened, and his shoulders relaxed. None of tonight should've turned out like it had, with her self-conscious around him.

"It's fine," she whispered, adding, "Your mom's probably at the inn making muffins and pastries for breakfast tomorrow before everyone leaves. The ranch house's kitchen is bigger than hers," she explained, then rolled her eyes. "But you already know that."

She was still covering herself.

"You don't have to hide from me, Cassie."

She nodded, new tears in her eyes. "It feels like I do."

A lump in his throat formed as he re-dressed.

He walked toward the front entryway where they'd shared one hell of a kiss earlier tonight. This time, Cassie's footsteps didn't follow. He grabbed his boots and cowboy hat, closing the door gently behind him, not wanting to wake Sunny. He couldn't turn back before the knob clicked. There was no good that would come from knowing what he was leaving behind this time.

He trudged through pain as thick as molasses as he started toward the inn. He wished Cassie could soothe him, but she had caused the damn trouble. He chuckled humorlessly as he walked. He'd once loved trouble with Cassie Sullivan. She was the sweetest kind.

He let the door literally hit him on the ass when he entered his childhood home. His mom was muttering to herself, back turned, as she tasted something on the stove.

"Mom—"

She spun and pointed the spoon like a sword. She lowered the weapon and clutched her chest. "You nearly gave me a heart attack."

He winced. "Don't say that."

She cast her eyes at the counter between them. "It's just a phrase."

He nodded, kicking his boots against the wood floor. His breaths weren't working right as he tried to control himself. He brought his fist to his mouth and bit his knuckle.

"Fuck," he muttered angrily against his skin. *Not*

here. Not now.

"Jacob Smith, it's time you break open." His mom walked over and pulled out the bench at the table, guiding him onto it. He put his hands on the wood and his forehead on his knuckles.

"I can't breathe." It was seven years ago all over again. The gut-punch of his dad dying; the life-altering moment when he was next in line for the family ranch prematurely; the spiral out of control with no compass to lead him.

The fact was, as much as Cassie had been his world that summer, he was always meant to lose her. Instead, he lost everything. He was constantly losing what mattered the most to him. Seven years of suppressing this shit was catching up to him.

"Mom, I can't breathe."

She rubbed his back. "You can."

He thought he'd broken down when he pursued a different path. But that wasn't breaking down. He left to avoid this moment. His sobs came easily, and they weren't quiet. They rippled through him like waves, crushing his soul. As much as he wanted to flee, his feet wouldn't move.

"I can't," he sobbed.

"You can," she answered. "You are."

****

He was depleted in a way he'd never been in his lifetime. He hiccupped after his sobs ceased. Two fucking hours he'd sat quietly moaning as his mom stared at him like an exotic animal. He'd stopped twice to go to the bathroom.

Early bird wedding guests were leaving, but they nodded quickly when they recognized their ill-timing.

He waved off a few overly curious neighbors as he pounded his head lightly against the table. His mom closed the door leading to the small dining area to preserve the last of his dignity.

"Jake," his mom said.

He finally lifted his head. He was dizzy.

"You need to let the truth settle before you process it. This all takes time." She sat across from him in her plaid pink pajamas that his dad had given her the Christmas before he'd passed away. She'd been oddly giddy about those damn pajamas. She still had her wedding brooch in her hair.

"Cassie and I were a fling. That's the truth." He stood because he had to do something. He reached for a knife and stabbed the cutting board on the counter.

"What did that board ever do to you?" His mom twisted on her seat. "Jake, look at me."

He reluctantly complied but kept his mouth in a firm line.

"You're not talking at all now?"

He shook his head.

"Fine. Then, I'll talk. Cassie wasn't a fling. You can stand there and fib to me all you want, but I'm going to call you out on it. That's my job, and you're finally here so I can tell you. You need to keep talking this through with her and your brother."

The thought of them together made him sick all over again. He only coughed into his fist this time. Progress. "What if I can't?"

"You can," she said as if it was that simple. "You make stupid choices when you don't communicate." She muttered, "stuntman," under her breath.

"Hey, you've seen my movies."

She pursed her lips. "To check in on you, sweetheart. I want you to be okay."

"I am okay."

She nodded. "Clearly."

Silence settled.

"I'm jealous," Jake admitted. "They took my life."

"Now we're getting somewhere." His mom walked to the opposite side of the counter. She shoved a fresh plate of cookies toward him and moved the injured cutting board away. A chocolate chip cookie sounded like a good idea.

"Frankie has quite the shiner because of your jealousy. Did you really hit him?" she asked as she went to the refrigerator. She retrieved milk, grabbed a glass from the cabinet and filled it half full, and pushed the glass toward him.

"He tattled on me?" Jake bit into half the cookie.

"He stopped over here before you did to tell me his big news."

Jake grumbled, "What news? That we fought?"

She smiled. "Kate's pregnant. Apparently Cassie already knows. I'm pretending not to be offended I'm the second in line to hear. Someone thinks I have a big mouth."

"You keep plenty of secrets." He didn't have the heart to tell her that she was at least third in line because he knew about the pregnancy, too.

"It was big of him not to ruin Missy's day," he added.

His mom put a new sheet of cookies into the oven. "Your brother's not bad, Jake. I raised him the same way I raised you."

He stared at the counter. "I should've fought for

the life I wanted. Dad would be ashamed of me."

"Did you know your father knew Cassie was pregnant the day he had his heart attack?"

Jake glanced up. "He did?"

She lowered her glasses down her nose, approaching the counter again. She'd put her lenses on somewhere around the time she'd started making cookies during his meltdown. "He found the pregnancy test in the bathroom. At first, he thought it was mine."

Jake grabbed his milk. "You were old."

She swatted at him even while they both laughed. "No, I didn't mean old, old. You're beautiful, Mom. But you were forty-eight, forty-nine?"

"Fifty-three." She settled into a smile and answered, "I said the same thing to your father."

"I take it Dad found out it wasn't you."

His mom wiped tears away. They could've been tears of laughter or from sad memories. "The day he died, Cassie was crying in her room, and your dad heard her. He didn't tell me exactly what she said to him when we talked an hour before he…"

The sentence didn't need to be completed.

She closed her eyes.

"Mom."

She shook her head. "He told me Cassie had confessed to taking the pregnancy test. We were relieved it wasn't Missy. Funny to think about that reaction now."

Jake moved around the counter and hugged her. She'd saved Cassie's life in many ways, and he'd repay her for it somehow. "What else did Dad say to Cass?"

She patted his back. "He said 'Jake is a good man. He's going to be a wonderful father and take care of you, Cassie.'"

A lump formed in his throat, and he backed away. "Sunny is Frankie's kid. Not mine."

"I'm sure your dad just assumed the baby was yours. Cassie didn't tell him any different, apparently." She left the room. When she returned, she had tissues in her fists and continued as if she hadn't left. "All I know is that girl has loved you from the night she spilt fruit salad on your pants."

"The first night." He smiled. "I remember."

He hadn't actually recalled that detail until she'd mentioned it.

"She was my biggest dream come true for you, my boy. She made you happy."

"I thought you wanted me to ranch," he said. "Then the family legacy would continue. It's our livelihood. Wasn't that your dream for me?"

"You loved ranching. That's why I liked when you did it." She picked up a cookie and broke it in half. "It's why your dad pushed you. Because you wanted to ranch, and he showed you the work that went into it. He would've sold the place to Uncle Randy if you would've wanted to do something else. We had those discussions, Jacob. Your dad and I had a plan."

Jake hadn't known it was an option to sell the property to his dad's brother.

"Why can't Cassie sell it to Uncle Randy now?"

"Have you seen your Uncle around this weekend?"

"No."

"He has MS. He's in a group home in Lincoln."

"Oh."

She sighed. "It's time to give someone else the opportunity to enjoy this place."

"Ranching did make me happy."

The sentence didn't feel right being in the past tense. Still, Jake had a lot of life to rewind, contracts signed, sealed, and delivered for several more stunt projects. He had a condo. He had friends in California, sort of. He couldn't keep running from the careers he built.

"Why didn't you ever chase me down, Mom?"

"I knew you missed your dad, and I couldn't bring him back for you." She paused, as if she was thinking to that time again. "And then I thought you left because Cassie told you about Frankie, and I couldn't blame you for being upset. I was livid when Cassie told me what they'd done. I was livid for you. Then I was mad when I found out you had no idea about Sunny, and you still weren't coming around. You'll learn this if you have kids someday. You have to let them make their own choices. You weren't hurting yourself going off on your own. I trusted you. I didn't like it, but you were and are an adult."

He rubbed his face. Time dulled people's senses. Did no one but him feel the hurt of what Cassie and Frankie had done? Everyone spoke of it like it was old news, and it was him who needed the fixing.

Because he did. That was the thing. A lot of time *had* passed.

Jake was devastated for a reason he didn't want to admit.

He was still in love with Cassandra Sullivan.

This shitshow would take a lot to get over.

"What is it about Cassie that you like, Mom?"

Her smile reached her eyes. "She's my daughter, as real to me as Missy is my baby. She's charming and kind and loving. She gave me my first grandbaby. I see her working her behind off on a dream that isn't even hers."

She eyed him.

"What?" Jake asked defensively. His chest tightened, and he rubbed it. Maybe the milk was too rich this early.

"A dream that isn't even hers," she repeated.

"A dude ranch isn't my dream, either," he argued. "She's hardly living out these dreams for me."

His mom rolled her eyes. "For such a smart man, you sure are a dummy sometimes. I think the poor girl is trying to hold onto this place because she's so darn afraid you'll regret the choices you've made. If that's not love, I don't know what is. How can I not adore her? She loves my son."

"She doesn't love me."

His mom pointed a single, strong finger at him. "You don't want her love to be true because it means you made a mistake. You're as stubborn as your dad, who I told to go to the doctor for months before his heart attack. When are men going to learn that women know best?"

Not today.

He left the room, scribbled on a notepad next to the landline, and pointed toward it afterward. "That's my new cell number."

"You're leaving?"

"I have a life to get back to." He sagged to the door.

"You should at least say good-bye to Cassie this time," she said to his back.

"My leaving proves my point enough. Maybe this

187

time she'll understand what it means. She should do what's best for her." Hurt was a powerful emotion. He couldn't feel past his own. Everything fucking hurt. "It's up to her and Frankie."

"You don't mean that."

"Yes, I do."

"Cut your hair." His mom scolded.

He let her have that much.

****

He left at noon on a gray but bright Sunday. The dust-colored clouds drifted over the landscape, making the grasses greener. The taller blades seemed to wave good-bye to him with the help of the breeze. A small, white bus was parked outside the stable. Early summer camp kids lined up excitedly, their shouts high, ready for dude ranch fun.

But ranching was hard work.

It was great work.

They'd learn the ropes because of Cassie.

He was proud of her; of everything she'd accomplished since they were younger. She was everything he knew she'd be—strong, capable, and fine without him.

The woman of his broken dreams.

Children's voices carried through the wind again, and his chest heated with tightness that reached his throat. He'd woken up every damn day on the Smith property as a child and young man with their same excitement for ranching life. Nothing had made him happier. Hours weren't hours when he was working the land. Time had passed by like seconds.

Much like this weekend. Where had it gone?

Sunny waved good-bye to him from the inn's front

porch. His most recent broken promise would probably hurt Cassie more than any other thing he'd messed up with her. His chest ached. Sunny was standing calmly—watching him leave, likely because she did the same thing with her father every time he left. She understood too young how people came and went from her life. It may not matter to her now, but it would eventually. His breakdown last night proved that much.

"Dammit." He swore under his breath. With his hand on his car door, he turned toward her.

"A couple throws?" he asked.

She nodded seven times in two seconds, nearly jumping off all three steps to get to the grassy front yard. She already had her glove. He caught the green ball with his bare hands. Neither of them talked for the twenty minutes they played, but it wasn't awkward, either. It was...nice. He didn't want to stop playing, but he finally had to so he didn't sob again. The lump in his throat was already nearly choking him. This wasn't his life. As natural as it felt, Sunny was Frankie and Cassie's child.

"Thank you, Jakey-boy." Sunny had likely overheard his nickname from Frankie. It sounded sweeter coming out of her mouth.

He didn't mind it from her. "You're welcome."

When she ran to him, he side-hugged her.

She stared, squinting because of the bright day. "You're my uncle?"

He hadn't thought about his relationship with Sunny yet. He'd simply regarded her as Cassie's kid with another man. But Sunny was his niece. All be damned. What a screwed-up family dynamic if he came to Christmas in the future.

He wouldn't hurt Sunny as badly if she never knew how much he loved her mom. However, he couldn't silence his love enough to reenter the family fold. He'd failed miserably this weekend already.

"Yeah, I'm your uncle." He put his arm around her shoulder again. His other hand fisted in his pocket. He was an uncle. He was Sunny's uncle.

"That means I'll see you more?" Sunny asked. "My friend, Kara, sees her uncles and aunties all the time. I'd really like that."

Whatever answer he gave had to be the truth. He wasn't going to make the same mistakes he'd made with Cassie. Sunny was an innocent child.

"Maybe." He crouched down.

She stood in front of him, mitt and hands clasped in a "pretty please" position under her chin. Her mouth was in a pout. She didn't have to squint now to see him.

He braced his fingers on the ground.

"Adult stuff is complicated."

"Because you love my mom."

Cover blown. "I love your mom very much, sweetheart."

"She loves you, too," Sunny said. "Sometimes when she thinks I'm asleep, I'm really awake. And I hear her talking to my dad. Did you know Frankie's my dad?"

Jake rolled his eyes. "I've heard, yes."

"Mommy tells him she loves Jake. You're Jake."

How could he explain something to a child that he couldn't even explain fully to himself? "Sometimes even when people love each other, they don't end up together."

"Why?" Sunny cocked her head.

"I don't know."

"That's stupid," she answered, as his mom called her in for lunch.

He straightened. Sunny waved and ran toward the house. When she reached her grandma—*shit*, his mom was her biological grandma—she hugged her, and they turned and walked inside.

He was still part of something in Lovestruck. He was an uncle, a brother, a son, an ex. It was a lot to absorb. It was too much. He cried as he drove down Main Street—past Lushes—and out of town. He wanted to burn the place down, and yet it had led to a little girl who was pretty damn awesome. He understood what Cassie had said about Sunny. How could he justify hating the facts while also kind of loving the outcome?

Frankie had done something right in helping create Sunny.

Jake had to pull over and dry heave out the driver's side window. It would take him a while to remove the goddamn boulder weighing down his chest. Perhaps he wouldn't succeed. He'd given the answer "maybe" to Sunny, so he hadn't lied. His life was one, big maybe right now.

Maybe he'd survive this. Maybe he wouldn't.

His cell phone rang.

"Hello?" His voice was clipped.

"Hey, Smith," his current agent, a petite woman named Carly, said. "You ready for next week?"

His newest project was his biggest stunt job to date in more than one way. Time. Money. Bravado. "Yeah, I'm all set."

His chest constricted.

He drove faster. "I'm ready."

His Lexus huffed, as if mocking him.

Chapter Eighteen

Jake

Jake grunted. The wires attached to his harness dug into his chest and shoulder blades. He jolted off the motorcycle under him, and the bike crashed into a set wall. A fake fire erupted on impact.

"Cut!" The director yelled. "That's a wrap for you, Smith."

His actor counterpart whooped praise behind the camera. Jake waited for someone to free him. Once his feet hit the ground, his assistant brought a bottled water. He grabbed a handful of grapes from the craft table on his way toward the parking lot behind the set. He popped the fruit into his mouth. Cassie drifted callously into his head. She'd been beautiful when she'd set the bowl of grapes on the table during Missy's wedding weekend.

That was three weeks ago.

His thoughts had trailed to Cassie every day since then. His greatest fear was that she'd always have a powerful hold on him. His bigger fear was that she wouldn't.

Their blowup in Lovestruck had been a doozy. His anger turned to pain everywhere in his body when he'd returned to California. Pain Cassie had caused; pain Frankie had caused; pain he'd caused.

Said pain had even conjured up an image of Frankie leaning against his car now.

Jake shook his head, but Frankie didn't dissipate. His brother walked toward him, stopping two feet away. He wore a dress shirt and slacks.

"What are you doing here?" The words were acid-laced when they came out of Jake's mouth. But his chest hurt like a horse's hoof had stomped on it. Acid-laced was an appropriate tone.

Frankie held up his hands much like he'd done when he'd tried to wrangle the cow in the barn. As if Jake was a wild animal needing to be tamed.

Jake cocked an eyebrow. "Seriously?"

"I just wanted to see if you were okay."

"It's a little late for your concern, Franklin."

Frankie dropped his hands. "I'm hoping not."

Silence filled the space between them, and Jake almost believed Frankie was a mirage again. He moved past him, keys in hand but dropped his bottled water when Frankie grabbed his bicep. The bottle rolled to his brother's feet.

Jake didn't bother picking it up. "You came a long way for nothing. I have no words for you."

He meant he had no words prepared. Given enough time, he could find something cruel and unforgiveable to say. Or he could ask how Cassie was doing. Had she cried when he'd left? Had Sunny told her they'd played ball together? Frankie likely knew those answers. The world was upside down in all the important ways, and Jake needed to avoid those places...forever. He'd done a good job of it until three weeks ago. Time would re-train him.

"Jake." Frankie sounded exactly like their dad.

Jake stared at his brother, whose bruise was no longer visible like their fight had never happened.

He still had his own scars. They ran much deeper.

"*I* have something to say." Frankie fisted his hands at his sides. He relaxed his fingers only when Jake didn't move.

"I'm sorry," Frankie started. "I hate this entire situation. I hate it hurt you. I hate it hurt Cassie. I hate I'm hurt, too, but I don't want us to never speak again over this."

Jake's nostrils flared. "Like we've ever had a good relationship in the past."

Frankie crossed his arms. "And why is that? I sure as hell have always loved you."

Jake gulped. It would take a shitload of pride to explain that he'd always felt inferior to his brother—second fiddle for not having the same want to travel across the country to find his life, even though it was what he'd ended up doing.

"You never gave me much attention," Jake answered. "Your mind was made up well before you left that you were too good for Lovestruck." He exhaled. "And for me."

"My dreams weren't in Lovestruck, Jake. What kind of job is there for a guy like me? What kind of life? You had the ranching gig down. There wasn't room for me, even if I was interested. Mom and Dad were fine with my path. Hell, Missy left Lovestruck. Why don't you punish her?"

Jake had never experienced the same rejection from Missy. He chalked it up to sibling dynamics. He idolized his older brother until he didn't. He couldn't remember exactly when the shift had happened. He'd needed his big brother more than he ever admitted.

Now, his big brother needed him. For forgiveness.

Frankie continued, "Dad and you always had a better relationship. I felt out of place when we were together. You talked his ear off about land, and it wasn't in my blood the same way it was in yours." He kicked at the parking lot pavement. "I still feel like the third wheel when it comes to Lovestruck."

"What's that supposed to mean?"

Frankie hit Jake upside the head. "Cassie is in love with you. And before you start thinking I love her, too, I don't. Not in the same way. She's Sunny's mother, and we've become friends. But she loves you, asshole. Why aren't you with her right now? For Christ's sake, live your life."

Jake pointed to set. "I have a life here, Frankie. A job...a...condo."

"Your heart is with Cassie, and you damn well know I'm right. She loves you and when a good woman like her gives you her love unconditionally, you hold onto it." Frankie's chest moved like rapid waters. He breathed solely through his nostrils. He wasn't a bull-like man unless it came to the markets, but he sure sounded like one now. Jake was impressed.

"Then why isn't she here telling me this?" he asked.

Frankie rolled his eyes. "Cassie came to California."

"When?" He wished there was a place to sit down. His legs were wobbly. "Recently?"

"About a year after Sunny was born and the dust had settled a bit. She bought a plane ticket and flew out to see you."

"What—uh—" Jake was dazed, as if he'd just fallen off a horse. "What happened?"

"You were at a premiere. She realized you had a new life, and she didn't want to bother you. She wasn't not fighting for you back then, brother. She was just trying to save herself after she saw you weren't coming home."

"And she never tried again?" It was a stupid question. The fact that Cassie had attempted to reach him at all melted something in his broody, sulking heart.

Frankie looked away. "I think she figured if she didn't talk to you, there was hope somehow. Time does amazing things to people's perspectives. For instance, you still love Cassie even though we have a daughter together. Why? Because what happened is in the past, Jacob. You can decide to heal from it. It's your choice. And you should try to heal because you and Cassie are not history. You're a forever thing. You and Cassie. *Timeless.*"

Jake gulped. "Holy shit. You're a fucking poet."

Frankie turned and patted his shoulder. "Among other things."

"Has she finally lost hope in me?" He wanted the easiest answer so they could all move on from this damn soap opera. There was a child involved—real consequences outside of their own feelings.

"Mostly," Frankie replied matter-of-factly. He took his sunglasses from his pocket and put them on. "And she doesn't know I'm here, either, so I'm not just a ploy to get information out of you."

Jake nodded. "I don't know whether I could've gotten over the news about Sunny if Cassie would've told me back then." Talking to his brother like an actual confidant was a strange rodeo.

"And maybe she'll never get over you abandoning her just like her parents did." Frankie had a new fight in his tone.

"I didn't—" He stopped. Had he abandoned her like her parents?

"You weren't there for Cassie," Frankie added when Jake didn't continue. "You became another person she couldn't count on. I've been that dick, too. Cassie is better than all of us with the forgiveness she gives away. She's amazing."

That was fucking true.

No matter how many ways he tried not to be affected by Frankie's last statements, the words gut-punched him. He'd disguised his actions in many different excuses, but the bottom line was he had let Cassie down in more ways than one. He was still letting her down. She deserved better.

Frankie moved toward his car, a Lexus. Jake chuckled humorlessly. He'd gone and done it. Turned into his older brother. And he still wasn't happy.

"Franklin," he yelled.

Frankie stared over the car's hood.

"Thanks for finding me."

"I'm rooting for you, Jake. Whatever it's worth, I'm not trying to tell you how to be happy. But I know Cassie does it for you. Dad's not here, so it's my job to remind you when you're being an ass." He winked. "Call me if you need anything."

He got into his car and drove away.

Jake watched him go, still not sure if he'd just experienced real life or another take from a movie. He had a lot to chew on, if he chose to chew on any of it. He had been one of the lucky ones born exactly where he could thrive. Guilt flooded through him like the hundred times it had before his brother's visit. When the pain in his chest subsided, two images remained imprinted in his mind—a cowboy hat and the prettiest brown eyes he'd ever looked into.

Timeless dreams.

Cassie was part of the pain he'd suffered for too many years, and she sure as hell would cause more pain as he healed. Could she be part of the solution, too? He didn't believe caring for someone—loving them—could conquer everything. There would be more fairy-tale endings in life if that were the case. What he did figure, standing alone in the parking lot of a movie set, was that anything was possible.

He kicked the gravel lazily.

Anything was possible. Even healing his heart.

Chapter Nineteen

Cassie

"You look beautiful," Cassie said, hands clutched to her chest. The young woman in front of her beamed as she gazed into the mirror. She'd chosen a fit-and-flare ivory gown with a sweetheart neckline. Even with the clamps to hold the dress in place, the shape accentuated her frame perfectly. Her alterations wouldn't be complicated.

She chalked and pinned the hem, and within a half-an-hour, mother and bride were out the door and she was alone at I Do Boutique. Ms. Cristian was on vacation again with her daughter and granddaughter. This week, they'd gone to the Happiest Place on Earth.

"Just you and me, Mr. Finch," she chirped to her bird friend.

The store phone rang.

She suspected it was Heidi who she'd interviewed with in New York several weeks ago, shortly after Missy's wedding. On her way back, she'd dropped Sunny at Frankie's until summer's end, testing if the arrangement might work in the future.

It was miserable without her little girl.

She set the fabric down and walked to the center counter.

"I Do Boutique, this is Cassie." She propped the

phone between her ear and shoulder while she marked a couple items she needed to order on Monday.

"Hi."

Her voice caught. "Jake."

"Sorry to call you at work. It's the only number I have."

"No. That's okay. Hi." She stopped writing and looked up as if he was in front of her.

It had been a month and six days since Jake left Lovestruck, and she'd arrived at the point where she was thinking about him roughly once an hour versus once a minute. When she wasn't thinking about him, there was a sense of him around her. Still, she hadn't expected to hear from him for at least seven more years, given his track record.

Shock filled her like a potted plant that was given too much water.

"What did you tell my dad when he found out you were pregnant?" he asked.

Her palms were so clammy she dropped the pen onto the counter. It bounced onto the floor.

"Who told you that?" Her mind rushed to the memory. Her mind rushed to the last moments with the Smith patriarch. In truth, there was only one person who would've told Jake about the conversation.

"Mom," Jake explained. "I had a long talk with her after the shit hit the fan after Missy's wedding."

"She mentioned you talked."

Bridget had told her that much, but she hadn't gone into details about the conversation. Cassie hadn't pressed. She'd been busy every week with visiting summer camps at the dude ranch and business at the boutique, on top of figuring out what she wanted to do with Sunny's and her life.

Frankie wasn't pressuring her to move, but it was his first choice, as it had been long ago when she was pregnant. However, she was trying to listen to her own heart and do what she truly wanted without considering a Smith brother. Of course, she was listening to Sunny, too, who loved Lovestruck, even though she was enjoying the east coast. Laying out her options was a strange freedom. Cassie was more liberated than she had been in a long time. She'd given herself the right to be happy. She wouldn't have Jake screwing anything up with this phone call. Even if his question seemed innocent.

"Your dad heard me crying the day you took me to the fourth of July festival." She paused. "The day he died."

"I searched my brain for weeks, trying to remember that night. I even went to a hypnotist to get the thoughts out of me," Jake said.

"Did it work?"

He started relaying details. "I'd insisted we treat our dates like 'real ones,' so I drove up the driveway and left flowers in the passenger side seat for you."

"Very good." She smiled and took the phone into her hand, giving her shoulder and neck a break. "That's true."

He continued. "I remember rides and cotton candy and mini-donuts. You got sick at one point."

She bit her bottom lip. "I figured it was from the tilt-a-whirl. Apparently, morning sickness is anytime sickness."

"I held your hair back."

"I told you not to look," she added. "I should've

confessed my getting sick wasn't from the ride."

"I should've let you," Jake answered like he'd been thinking about it a lot. His words were at the ready. "You were quiet that night. I asked you if you were okay."

"I really was going to tell you," she explained. "I didn't want to hurt you, but I wanted to be honest. Please know that. It was my intention to tell you. I had to talk to Frankie first though." She half-laughed. "None of it went as planned obviously."

His voice lowered. "The ambulances passed us and something bigger engulfed our lives. I forgot you never answered my question."

"And a hypnotist helped you remember all that? Hope you paid her well."

"She started the process. It's amazing what you can remember when you make yourself do it." He took a drink of something.

She heard the gulp. "That must've been awful for you—telling my dad."

Jake's voice broke over the phone.

Her throat dried. She ached to hug him. As much as she was hurt by everything they'd gone through, she'd processed it a long time ago. She could even put the fact they had sex last month into the context of a proper good-bye. It was a beautiful moment; it was a beautiful weekend they'd both needed. Jake had only started to deal with the past, however. He had a long road ahead of him.

"It was hard, Jake. I told him how much I loved you and didn't want to hurt you. Honestly, I was more worried about losing you than I was about being a parent so young."

"You told my dad I wasn't the father?" He gulped loudly again.

"Yeah." She bent down to pick up the pen from the floor. She doodled on the Order Form she'd been filling out.

"Mom said he told her how wonderful a father I was going to be," he confessed.

"He must have figured you'd stay," she said. "I don't know. You would've been a great father, Jake. He believed you could handle the truth maybe. I didn't."

She heard loud breaks and a honk.

"Fuck."

"Are you okay?" Her heartbeats quickened.

"I'm fine. I just ran a stop sign," he said, adding, "So my dad knew?" he repeated. I'll be damned.

"Yes. Why?"

"It's another way I failed him."

"Jake?"

"Yeah." He sounded like a child, his vulnerability palpable.

"Your dad was proud of you. You didn't betray him by not taking over the ranch."

"He wouldn't be proud of this mess."

"You listen to me, Jacob Smith. I have a mom who decided to be resentful of my existence, and a father who decided he agreed when he abandoned me because I was my mom's kid. I recognize when parents love their children unconditionally. Your dad loved you as unconditionally as I love Sunny. She could aspire to being a chalk artist for the rest of her life, and I'd be proud of her."

"I don't think she'll be a chalk artist," he answered. "More likely a pro athlete."

A pause followed.

Her doodle was Jake's name in bubbled letters. "Sunny told me you played catch with her before you left. Thank you."

"I promised her I would," he said simply.

She shivered. He'd kept his promise to her daughter. Why did he have to be such a good but messed up man?

"Can I explain something, Jake?"

He didn't answer, so she repeated, "Jake?"

She heard his car door open and slam.

"I just got back to the set."

She sighed. His life was so different than hers. "Do you need to go?"

"Jake, we need you in three," someone yelled.

"What did you want to tell me?" he asked.

"Even before you came back last month, I'd forgiven you."

"And that's what your forgiveness looked like?" He chuckled.

"Hey, we kissed. And had sex." Cassie smiled. "It was pretty great."

"True."

She bit her lip. "No, truthfully, I have forgiven you. Sunny wasn't your responsibility, and it took me a long time to stop blaming you for abandoning a life that wasn't yours anyway. You chose to leave, and that was okay. It's what you needed to do. I left a life behind in Connecticut as a young adult. Friends, family. I came here. I started over because I couldn't handle my mom's public fall from grace. I get it. I get feeling like you have no place to just…scream."

"I still abandoned *you*," he said. "Even though I

always thought you'd go back to Connecticut with Missy, you didn't leave first. I did. I broke us up."

"I'm not quite done being angry at you for that yet." She laughed lightly. "But you've done well for yourself. You did beautifully at your sister's wedding. We had our closure."

"Jake." Someone called again.

"I know you tried to reach out, Cassie. You came to California after I left." His voice was rushed.

"A long time ago, Jake."

"Thank you for trying. It's more than I did, Cass."

Then fix it. She rubbed her forehead.

"Jake!"

"I have to go," he said. "I'm jumping off a building in five minutes."

"Sounds scary," she replied. But it wasn't as scary as her next three words. "Good-bye, Jacob."

"Don't say it like that," he said. "Like this is over."

She closed her eyes and pinched the bridge of her nose. She was done fighting for the story her heart wanted. She was over it. "Sometimes people who love each other don't end up together. But we've all survived, and that's what's important."

"Did Sunny tell you that?" he asked.

"No, she didn't."

She glanced up when a car door slammed and cursed for wishing he was outside. Instead, a mother and daughter parked, probably her next appointment. She fisted her hand and brought it to her forehead again. She could handle missing him forever. What she couldn't handle was his inability to make a grand gesture; his inability to come home.

She had frozen his life as best as she could. She

was tired, and he wasn't coming back. Furthermore, he wasn't in any of the plans she was sorting through now. She didn't want phone calls like this ruining her future.

He was a hopeless case.

"I'm taking the job in New York if I get it. I have to." She hung up as the bell over the door chimed. Oh God. She'd put an answer out into the universe.

But making a choice? It was a good thing.

"Welcome to I Do Boutique, home of happily ever after's." She smiled through the pain. Happily ever after didn't exist for her. Not yet or not anymore. She wasn't sure which would be her fate, and the answers weren't on her radar. She'd build her story a different way. That was what strong women did. They took heartbreak and made it meaningful. They took pain and submitted to it wholly, letting it transform them. She would be okay.

Bring on the bullshit. She could wrangle anything.

Only it would never be with Jake Smith by her side.

Chapter Twenty

Jake

Jake called Frankie. Cassie's good-bye over the phone had solidified his need to man up; to fight for something; to win her back. He hadn't slept in days, thinking of all the ways he needed to get his shit together. Quickly.

There had been a long list of things to do and people to make mad. Still, with every decision he followed through on, he was a little freer to follow the path he was dead set on walking now. Furthermore, he wasn't going to let Cassie give up on their story. It took time to bring closure to his current life, but he was resolute.

He was scared shitless his plan wouldn't work, however.

"Answer your damn phone, Frankie," he said to the ringtone.

His brother answered after the seventh long buzz. "Franklin Smith speaking, ready to help you build your wealth."

"Frankie, it's me." He wrote numbers on an ivory envelope he'd recently received. He was adding up figures for this call. Boxes were stacked behind him in his living room, and the stool he sat on at his kitchen counter was the only piece of furniture left in the condo he owned until the end of the month.

"I take it you got my number from Mom." Frankie was neither warm nor cold. Still, his tone felt like square one again.

How many times did he have to start over to get things right?

"Daddy, look!" Sunny said in the background.

"Are you in Lovestruck?" Jake asked, suddenly jealous.

"No. Why?" Frankie laughed at something Sunny had apparently done. "Great job, kiddo."

"Sunny," Jake said. His brother really was stupid. In the past, he would've teased him, but he was an evolving man. Plus, he needed his big brother.

Maybe Cassie had gone to the east coast to finalize her move. Whether she admitted it or not, the coast held her roots. Jake didn't blame her for taking the job in New York. However, he was hoping she might like what he was planning better.

"Sunny's staying with me for the rest of the summer. She got paint all over Kate." He paused, like he was listening to another person on his end. "Yes, Kate. I will help in a second." He paused. "It's Jake."

"Jakey-boy!" Sunny yelled loud enough for Jake to hear.

"Tell Sunny hi."

"I will," Frankie answered. "I only have a couple of minutes. Kate needs my help. This pregnancy is getting rough over here."

"Congratulations on the kid again. The new kid, that is." He ran his hand through his newly cut hair. "And Sunny, too."

"Thanks, Jake." Frankie sighed. "I wish we could

just move past this awkwardness."

Jake nodded even though Frankie couldn't see it. He was getting used to the idea his brother had a child with his ex. It would never not bother him, but it was something he had to manage because he'd made up his mind, and he hoped he could convince Cassie to change hers. She hadn't tried to call him after their phone call.

Jake quit his movie that day.

He would be paying for his other broken contracts for the next several months.

He'd also cut ties with his agent, which went over about as well as a child not getting ice cream for dinner. However, it was time to retire his stuntman life. He'd pulled off the greatest stunt of all by pretending his heart hadn't belonged with Cassie this whole time. He couldn't do it anymore.

"I got your and Kate's joint baby shower invite."

"And?" Frankie was apparently playing dumb.

"One of you knuckleheads addressed the envelope to Cassandra Sullivan and Jacob Smith."

"Did we?" Frankie asked. "Must have been a slip of the pen."

He chuckled. "I can see why your clients love you."

"I want you to do right by yourself," Frankie said. "Since I have you on the phone, I'll mention that Cassie is putting the land up for sale tomorrow. Mom's handling it mostly, as it's been pretty hard on Cass."

"Mom told me when I called a couple days ago." Jake had called her specifically about the land, in fact. He'd needed information on what Cassie was selling it for and how the property had been maintained over the past seven years. She had refused to tell him any of

Cassie's other plans.

"When is Cassie moving?" he asked his brother.

Frankie answered, "She told Heidi to give her a couple more weeks to decide about the job. She'd said yes initially but pulled back a day later because Sunny was struggling with relocating permanently. I feel for her. It's a big choice. They may stay at Mom's as she decides. That is, if the land sells quickly. At this point, if they do move to New York, Sunny will be starting school late, so that's not ideal."

"You want her to take the job," Jake said.

"I do, but I care about my daughter loving Lovestruck, too," his brother answered. "I also like the idea of them being close to Mom. It's easier for me to make the trip home, and Kate loves visiting small towns. We'd make it work. We've done well the past couple of years with creating more consistency."

It was big of Frankie to be thinking of all the variables. Jake admired the shit out of him. He was making sacrifices for the greater good. Like a hero. Like an older brother.

"I don't want her to move," Jake said.

"Well, Jake, too bad. I'm proud of her for doing something."

Jake tapped his finger on the counter. "Me, too."

He was happy for her.

"Do you want some advice?" Frankie offered, interrupting his thoughts.

"Sure."

"Cassie's waiting for you to make a grand gesture, despite all her 'being done with you' talking. Women love the grand gesture. You need to put your balls on a silver platter and man up."

Jake straightened on his stool like he was riding a goddamn horse across the country to win his woman back. He was resolved to do what he had to—rejection be damned. "That's why I'm calling. I need your help, Frankie."

Frankie laughed. "My help with putting your balls on a platter? I don't know."

Jake grumbled. This groveling stuff was tough. "I heard you're pretty good at numbers, and I'd like some guidance. I also need you to call Mom and negotiate with me. She's being one hard businesswoman, making sure I'm serious about my proposition."

"Maybe she just wants us all to talk more," Frankie admitted.

"That sounds like Mom," Jake answered. And it also sounded like a good idea.

After an hour of questions and answers, Frankie concluded the conversation with, "I can't believe you're doing this."

"Are you saying that as a good thing or a bad thing?" He stood from his stool. His ass was asleep, but the rest of him was live-wired.

"It's what you should've done a long time ago," Frankie said. "Could've saved us all a lot of trouble."

"You had a baby with the love of my life." Jake reminded him, attempting to be okay with it. He didn't dry heave at least. "That's a lot of trouble, too."

"Someday you'll laugh at the stupidity," Frankie answered.

Jake didn't think he'd get there, but he'd attempt anything for Cassie. "Okay, I'm doing this."

"You sure are," his brother answered as if they were in a sport's huddle. "Good luck, baby brother."

"Frankie?"

"Yeah."

"If this works, are you sure you're okay that Sunny isn't closer to you?" He paused, forming the words. "You are her father."

"Is it ideal for me? No. But none of this really is. If Sunny is happy, then I'm happy. It's a damn strange situation, but it's our reality. That simple."

"That simple." Jake tried to believe his brother's logic.

Frankie chuckled. "Yes, Jakey-boy, I'm lying, but I'm trying."

"You're a good man, Franklin." His voice was hoarse. He meant every word. Frankie was more like their dad than Jake ever gave him credit for because he'd been too busy picking on him.

"You're a good man, too, Jake."

****

Two months and one day after Jake left Lovestruck, he got his Chevy from the storage garage, packed it up, and drove out of California with one destination in his mind.

Not a state.

Not a city.

The star on his map wasn't a star at all.

It was a heart.

One beating heart.

He made one detour, and he hoped she liked the surprise.

Balls on a platter, coming right up.

Chapter Twenty-One

Cassie

The note Cassie found on her door after church had only four words.

Meet me in town.

No punctuation. No "hey there" or "sincerely."

The handwriting resembled Jake's.

Her heart pounded so hard she heard it in her ears. She glanced around the property from her porch. The Smith land was in front of her; the place she'd recently put up for purchase and which had sold immediately. A gentle breeze made the grass sound like ocean waves. Birds chirped to one another. The sun shone so brightly that the green of the land looked more yellow-ish—like she was actually living on the sun.

"God, this place is beautiful," she whispered. Her stomach hurt, but she chalked it up to the fact that no human liked change. Still, change brought the most beautiful adventures. All of her best days in life began when something shifted in her universe. What she couldn't seem to change, however, was her frustration over how he still infiltrated into her everyday life. Like now with the note.

Did the scribbles really look like his handwriting?

Most people in town had chicken scratch for penmanship. Hardly original.

More likely, Ms. Cristian needed help at the boutique and had forgotten to sign the note or tell Cassie to stop by when they'd seen each other after church. In fact, Ms. Cristian had been strange today, fumbling over her words to Cassie. The note wasn't from Jake.

No one had died.

No one was getting married.

No one had given birth to a child without telling him.

Cassie hadn't changed out of her Sunday dress. She put her hair into a low bun because of the heat. Despite the weather, she walked into town instead of driving. The movement of her feet against gravel soothed her, along with the smell of tall grass and small town existence.

Life had moved forward again.

Main Street was a fifteen-minute walk from her front door, and the road was stamped with painted stars and little fire sparks, a rival to the hearts that Valentine, Nebraska touted. She'd followed the path many times in the past seven years, and her chest still expanded with a sense of belonging. She may've not belonged with him, but she was a part of his hometown.

She was at peace saying "no" to the job opportunity in New York. Frankie had been all right with it, too. Much more than he had been when she initially wobbled with her decision.

She yearned to do more with her fashion design background, but ultimately, she couldn't raise her daughter on the east coast. Now, she hoped the sale of the Smith property would garner enough money to pay down her debt and finally buy into Ms. Cristian's succession plan quicker at the boutique. Cassie hadn't asked for the details about the Smith property sale, but Bridget had told her the buyer paid a third over the asking price. And he wanted to turn the land back into a traditional ranch.

Cassie wouldn't have it any other way.

Unfortunately, the sale made her homeless sooner than she'd anticipated, especially since she'd opted out of the New York job at the last minute. She and Sunny were staying with Bridget until she figured out what was next. She hated having to lean on Bridget yet again, but this time, it truly would be short-lived.

"Mommy!"

Did she will Sunny home?

She stopped, tears erupting from her eyes. Sunny, who she swore had grown several inches, ran toward her from the sidewalk outside the small strip mall where I Do Boutique was.

Cassie hugged her and spun her. "What are you doing back here early, sweetheart?" Her heart pounded. As if she'd walked here from the coast. "I was flying out to pick you up next week."

"Uncle Jakey-boy came to visit at Daddy's, and we all drove here in his truck. Daddy's with Bridg-Bridg. Kate stayed in Boston because she's setting up for her shower."

All Cassie heard was, "Uncle Jakey-boy."

That's when she noticed Jake's Chevy—the old truck with great memories—parked halfway on the curb in front of Ms. Cristian's boutique.

He'd kept it.

She set her daughter down, grabbed her hand, and walked toward the rusty red truck she'd known well.

Her fingers glided along its dusty exterior as she stared confusedly at the storefront of I Do Boutique.

Ms. Cristian's wooden sign had been replaced with a new one made of marble. Etched in elegant lavender calligraphy was Sunnyside Sewing and Fashion. The "g" at the end of "sewing" was curled up into a thread and needle.

"Oh my God," she whispered, one hand shading her eyes from the sun. Nearby, Sunny played with the baseball she took from her pocket.

"You don't like it?"

That voice.

Jake came up from behind her, the sound of his boots—not Sperry's—dragging distinctively against the pavement. He stopped next to her. His arm brushed hers, and her body relaxed.

"Am I in trouble for leaving again?" he asked, a lightness in his voice.

She nodded slowly, her eyes still on the sign. Jake was in so much trouble. She tried to seal her heart but seeing him fought every instinct except for one.

She wanted to hug him. To make sure he was real.

"What is this?" She faced him. God, he was beautiful. Dressed in a black T-shirt and jeans molded perfectly to his body. He wore his ivory cowboy hat, his blond hair peeking out from underneath—freshly cut but still long. He was tan. He was tall. He was muscled and toned but less bulky than he'd been when she last saw him.

"What is this?" she repeated. "And why do you look like a cowboy again?"

He smiled shyly. "It's not all processed yet, but let's just say I made Ms. Cristian an offer that allowed her to retire from her shop immediately."

"But she loves this place," Cassie's heart tightened, and she fought back tears. "She didn't want to sell yet. That's why her price was too high."

"She loves spending time with her grandbaby more." Jake took off his cowboy hat. She snatched it and put it on her head in an attempt to turn back time to when he had taught her the ways of ranching.

"I have to ask you to make a deal with me, too," he continued.

She crossed her arms. "I'm listening."

"I talked to Mom about the ranch. We negotiated something."

"You…you did? You're the crazy buyer who paid too much for the property?"

"I wouldn't call it crazy."

She bit her lower lip. "Why did you do it?"

"I'm ready to have my dreams back. With the loan Frankie helped me get, and some of my stunt work money getting dusty even after my deal with Ms. Cristian, I could pay you handsomely. Plus, I can continue to pay you in more than one way. That is, if you'll move in with me." He shrugged. "What do you say, Cassie? Please stay home. You've taken beautiful care of it. It's my turn now."

She shook her head. This moment wasn't happening; it only happened in her dreams.

"Please." His begging was beautiful.

Tears fell down her cheeks.

"Jake—"

He rambled, "I think it's great what you've done with the place. You breathed a different life into it and allowed people to see just how important ranching is to communities. I'd like to keep that part of the dude ranch idea—the horseback rides and education classes and then expand it into a working ranch again, too."

"You worked on this plan with Frankie?" she asked. "You guys made amends?"

He frowned. "I'm telling you I want you to be with me, and you're focused on the fact I made up with my brother?"

She shook her head. This man, almost eight years older than when she'd met him, was coming home asking for the life that was always his—the life she'd preserved for him stupidly. In all ways, she'd moved on from being the girl who'd first come to Lovestruck. Now, he was asking her to buy into their love story again.

The truth was, she'd pay anything for it.

"I love you, Cassie Sullivan," he added, as if he needed to throw in a sweetener. "Stay with me. Be with me."

She dipped Jake's hat lower onto her head and peeked at him from underneath the rim. The sight was worth it. Jake. Smiling. She hadn't witnessed his smile so wide since they were younger. "I didn't take the job in New York."

"Really?"

She nodded.

"Why?"

She paused. "For myself. I was excited for something new, but I chose a different dream a long time ago—to root myself where I landed. To be happy, Jake. I'm happy here. Sunny's happy here. I don't want to long for something I already have. Home."

"What do you say, then?"

She stepped toward him, brushing his torso with her chest. She reached up and placed his hat back on his head. "You have yourself a deal, cowboy."

His eyes widened. "Really? I've got more balls on a platter if you want."

"Balls on a platter?" She laughed. "You think I'd play hard to get right now? I love you, Jacob Smith. I've said that a thousand times in your absence hoping you could hear me."

"I'm sorry for running." His voice trailed off. "I really am."

Cassie nodded. "You broke my heart, and that matters. But you're here now, and dammit, that matters more."

"You sound so strong." He held her hands.

"It took time, Jake."

Time.

Time was a beautiful thing.

Chapter Twenty-Two

Jake

Time, Jake learned, was a tricky thing. It didn't heal all wounds, but time did at least make it a little easier to begin again, and maybe, and only sometimes, love became the best version of itself because of it.

"God, I love you." He leaned down and kissed her, finding her hand blindly and placing the keys to her boutique into her palm. She clenched them as she laced her arms around his neck and jumped, wrapping her legs around his waist.

He grunted not from the weight of her body but from the gravity of this moment—the past and future colliding. His goal would be to string along as many moments like this as possible. *Ordinary moments.*

"You promise you won't leave again?" she asked.

He smiled. "Well, I don't know, a career as a country singer sounds interesting. Maybe someday."

She slapped his chest, and he nestled his head against her shoulder.

She whispered, "Swear to me."

"I swear I'm not going anywhere." He kissed her collarbone.

"Good because there's one thing I haven't told you." She smirked, hopping onto the ground.

He eyed her as if he'd seen a snake crawl into his

boots. This woman's frightening power over him was humbling. And what's more, he was utterly okay with it. "What haven't you told me?"

"I actually learned to lasso, cowboy. I could catch you any day of the week. So now that we've made our deal, you're stuck with me forever."

"Sounds perfect." He picked her up again and spun her in his arms. Her sandals flew off her feet, landing somewhere on the pavement behind them.

He really didn't stand a chance this time, and he didn't need the chance anyway.

He came back to Cherry County for a reason.

For her and for her daughter.

For his family.

Epilogue

Cassie

"It's right there." Cassie pointed to a plot near the front fence of the church's property. The winter sun shone bright, and her skin was warm despite the sheet of ice that had frozen across the land last night. Typical December weather.

Mass had ended two hours ago, and Jake lingered behind—confessing he didn't want anyone to be part of this reunion except for her.

"I need you." He turned and held out his hand before approaching the stone. Their footsteps crunched along the icy grass walkway. Jake's dad's name was boldly but simply etched on its marker, along with his birthday and death day.

Jake brushed his fingers across the dash between the years as he crouched down. She stood behind him, resting her palms on his shoulders to anchor him to this moment.

A silent tear rolled down her cheek. She pursed her lips to keep herself together as Jake's body shook underneath her hands. He didn't acknowledge it afterward. Instead, he stood and wrapped his arm around her, kissing her temple and whispering, "The dash is all that matters in this life."

She glanced at the gravestone. "Yeah, and your dad

had one heck of a good dash."

He brushed his lips against her mouth. "I don't really care what mine looks like in the end, just as long it includes you every day."

She rested her head against his chest, listening to his heartbeat as she glided her fingers between their torsos, rubbing her belly. Her wedding ring sparkled in the sun. She loved catching glimpses of it—the round stone, the rose gold band. Traditional with a twist.

"All your days will include me," she said softly. "And Sunny."

"And cute-as-hell Sunny." His voice was affirming.

She stepped away and breathed lightly. "And another little one next summer."

"What?"

She nodded at his confused-turned-wide-eyed expression.

His chest rose and fell as he pulled her toward him again. "You're—"

"We're having a baby," she said. The words were less scary this time around.

His eyes glassed over with tears, and he didn't sniff them away as he rested his forehead against hers. He wanted to express everything to her. To feel every goddamn sensation from the news…he was going to be a dad.

He brushed her coated arms with his bare fingers. "My heart's beating so fast."

"Mine, too."

"We're having a baby, Cassie?" He hugged her.

She smirked. "We are. May he or she be as stubborn and broody as you, cowboy."

Jake kissed the top of her hatted head as she rested her palms on his chest, savoring the moment.

"Thank you for letting it be me this time."

Cassie pulled away and stared at him. "It was always you, Jake. This family. This life. It's always been yours."

"Ours," he answered.

She smiled. "Ours."

A word about the author...

Laura is a lover of all things romance. She's a former student of the Gotham Writers Workshop in New York and an on-going student at The Loft Literary Center in Minneapolis, Minnesota. After participating in PitchWars in 2015, Laura continued writing love stories. Strong heroes and heroines are a must.

Her short story "Ohhhh Holy Night" was published in Fuse Literary's annual *Hot Holiday Reads* anthology (2015). Her romance fan-fic "Still A Little Bit Famous" was listed in LitRejection's annual short story contest (2016). Her YA short story "After We Survive This" was included in an anthology by Indomita Press. (Sadly, this work was not romance). She earned honorable mention in the Writer's Digest 86th, 87th, and 88th Annual Writing Contests (2017-2019) for her work in romance.

In her spare time, she teaches yoga, enjoys hiking, and talks often with her writer friends, whose group name is inappropriate for public consumption.

Check Laura out on Instagram at:
        lauraelizabethwrites
or Twitter:
        @lauraeliz529

Thank you for purchasing
this publication of The Wild Rose Press, Inc.

For questions or more information
contact us at
info@thewildrosepress.com.

The Wild Rose Press, Inc.
www.thewildrosepress.com